The Boys' House

The Boys' House

Stories by
JIM HEYNEN

Introduction by
BILL HOLM

MINNESOTA
HISTORICAL
SOCIETY
PRESS

www.mnhs.org/mhspress

Manufactured in the United States of America.

10 9 8 7 6 5 4 3 2 1

International Standard Book Number
0-87351-413-0 (cloth)

♾ The paper used in this publication meets the minimum
requirements of the American National Standard for
Information Sciences—Permanence for Printed Library
Materials, ANSI Z39.48-1984.

Library of Congress Cataloging-in-Publication Data
available upon request.

The Boys' House

Introduction

A small-souled demon lives inside the body of American culture—either literary or otherwise. When it hears news, for instance, that another of Jim Heynen's books of tales is about to appear, it rolls its dry tongue behind its tight pincer lips and croaks: "Regional!" By which it means, provincial; by which it means: grass, pigs, farmers, sloughs, chickens live inside these pages. They come from flyover-land, somewhere five miles below the machine that carries them from Manhattan to media-ville and back again. Sioux Center, Iowa, indeed! Where are the terrible childhoods, the bored fathers, the sour love affairs, the angst, the irony, the whine? How can literature presume to wisdom, wonder and pleasure, without a therapist or a broker for a thousand miles? Regional! That's what it is! Off with its head.

This croak damaged the literary careers of a legion of splendid writers from the "provinces," Jim Heynen's fellow Dutchman, Fred Manfred, among them. But what does the demon imagine a "province" to be? Somewhere with trees, fields, farmers where plain English—the hardest of all to craft—is spoken and read, expected to carry metaphor and beauty inside it. It is the old ritual literary war between city and country, pastoral and urban that has been puttering along for centuries. Jim Heynen's genius is to find literature on a farm. There's the bald fact. What he finds, however, is amazingly original, sly and sophisticated in both form and content. He finds, like his old countrymen Thoreau and Mark Twain, the whole universe laid out before him in a barn.

I first discovered Jim Heynen's work in the fall of 1980. I had just returned from two years teaching in Iceland, after a long stretch on the East Coast, and made a conscious choice to be a Midwesterner again. My literary mentors: Robert and Carol Bly and Fred Manfred lived here, a new college full of writers had opened in Marshall. I took a job teaching creative writing and settled in. The neighbor college in Brookings, South Dakota, hosted a fall prairie literary conference, so I drove 50 miles west down the road with a carload of students and my old friend John Allen—

a wandering storyteller and my fellow Minneotan. We had a good time and heard splendid poetry readings: David Allen Evans, Bill Kloefkorn, and Ted Kooser among them, as I remember. As with all such events, this one had a special little bookstore set up to peddle the work of local writers. Years before, I took a private vow to always buy at these stores, (aside from writers I knew or had heard) one book by a writer completely unknown to me, selected on the basis of title alone. I forbade myself from opening the book to see whether it was good or bad. Just eye the title, cough up the cash, and open it only when it's too late to get your money back. Writers need buyers after all. Take a chance. It's a better deal than the lottery.

I spotted *The Man Who Kept Cigars in His Cap*, a slender gray book with a cover drawing of an old farmer sitting in front of a barn. $5.00 cash. We left in late afternoon to drive east down Highway 19 through the rolling autumn prairies, now half tan, half pale orange. My old friend John drove. I opened *Cigars*, probably said something like: "We'll see if this Heynen fellow is any good." I flipped through the book at random stopping at "Fewer Cats Now." I read it aloud.

John laughed with such violence that he pulled to the shoulder of the road. "Another," he demanded. I read "Ducks and Bacon Rind" on the facing page. He pulled to the shoulder again. "Good, eh?" "Good." At "Bloating and its Remedies" we headed for the ditch, but stopped in time. I read "Strange Smells in the Night." The whole car sighed in unison. We worked our way back to the title piece, a haunting story about the enormous claims made on human beings both by Nature with a capital N, and by our own frail sometimes mean-spirited human nature. After 50 miles, we traveled in a car full of Heynen fans.

But what was this odd book? The title page gave no help. Prose poems? Tales? Fables? Parables? As with all the best American books, Heynen's work fits no clear academic genre category. His "tales" rarely exceed two pages, so it can be safely said that they are short. Some are pure image, some pure narrative, some jokes, some fables, some are lyrical (the goose lady), some pure comedy, some are political (the old saw-sharpener), some theological. Whatever exists in the world exists as well in these page-long "things." To settle the question, I call them "Heynens." Heynen doesn't call them that, but he may not tell you what he calls them either.

If you take Whitman seriously—"Who touches this book touches a man"—then you track down the author of books so full of delight that they almost drive you into a ditch on a clear dry Autumn day. I found Heynen the next summer in Port Townsend, Washington, on the Straits of Juan de Fuca, and demanded that he buy me a drink for having tried to wreck my car. He did. We sat on his porch talking. How strange, I thought, this Iowa Dutch farm boy with a wry wit and a first-class eye for the telling details of human frailty surrounded by jogging, veggie, new-age, west-coast life-stylers who wouldn't know a Hereford from a Holstein or corn from beans. Yet they understood that their neighbor was a writer of size and power who had invented his own peculiar window into the mystery of human experience. Maybe the demon was wrong. Maybe true literature is always "local," always regional, always provincial. Heynen, for all that, has now made his way back to the Midwest where he belongs, and for that we ought all to be grateful.

Where do these tales take place? Iowa is never named; nor are the characters: "the boys" and "the men." Considered from one angle, "the boys" may not even be a gang, but only the prisms of light that travel through a single consciousness, acquiring the world and having arguments with itself. "The men" may not be multiple either, but only the voice of country middle-aged prudence trying to protect itself from any more surprises. The grandfather speaks the voice of the old country, thus history and the invisible world of the imagination. Uncle Jack is the voice of pure magic, the holy fool who finds wisdom and beauty in the world of play. "Uncle Jack and the Beautiful School Teacher" seems to me one of the masterpieces of pure lyricism in American literature—two of the loveliest pages I know.

Heynen also finds theology on his farm. He was trained in the strict Calvinist tradition, and while, like most writers, he has left childhood orthodoxy behind him, an essential orthodoxy survives in his work. He practices Wonder in the old sense. The boys who go to a neighbor to ask for apples find him "praying to his animals." He is not an object of fun, but rather an instrument for teaching the holiness of the ordinary. Who is "The Great Strength?" Maybe the mysterious breath of the divine, blowing past human beings to remind them of something large and invisible in their lives.

Some tales satirize the cautious timidity of a small-minded peasant culture that expects rigid conformity of its members. "Who are those people anyhow? They drive Studebakers instead of Fords, plant Pioneer instead of Dekalb." We *are* our goods. Our habits define us—and shrivel us.

The boys discover true Eros on the farm, too. In "The Boys Learn by Watching" the old men are tenderly rubbing a sow's teats to see if she is ready to farrow. "When the men left, the boys tried it and knew they were doing it right when the sow's low grunting sounded the same as when the men were rubbing her." This was "a secret that would always be there when they needed it."

In the title story of this collection, "The Boys' House," Heynen uses architecture as metaphor. The boys weary of what wearies all of us in the modern, high-tech world of money-making. Nature itself disappears: no silence, no darkness, no smell of grass, so the imagination finds itself homeless, downsized to the bottom line, sliced off at the cutting edge. The boys assemble junk, whatever the twentieth century threw away as without use or value. They construct an eccentric combination pleasure dome and monastic retreat by a farm pond. Inside they find nature again and make a safe house for the imagination. All Heynen's books of tales are "boys' houses" like this—odd looking contraptions into which you are invited when you want to live without the noise and cant of modern life for a while.

So if God, Eros, ethics and the imagination live on this farm, what objection can the anti-regional demon make to it? Is Eros richer in New York, God happier in California? Are we so sunk as a culture by marketing and cyberspace that we can no longer recognize real literature when it is spread out on a page before us?

For years I have been giving Jim Heynen's books to my neighbors, relatives, ordinary people who do real work in the world—aside from literary criticism. Many have been so bamboozled by bad teaching, brainless media and hierarchical literary puffery that they say to me: "That can't be literature. I liked it and understood it. But whatever you call it, get me another one of his books if it is that good." So I do. Now, thanks to the Minnesota Historical Society Press, I will be able to have so many wonderful old stories too long out of print, and a goodly number of new ones to give them. Jim Heynen has invented a fine window through which to look into the shadowy corners both of nature and consciousness for a page or two at a time. May he go on having his look for many more books full of them.

BILL HOLM

To my family and all rural families
who are trying to keep farm life and its stories alive

The Boys' House

1

That Could Have Been You

The boys knew that on the farm danger was everywhere, sometimes in the teeth of a spinning gear,
other times in the jaws of a growling boar. Danger
could plunge from the sky in jagged-edged hail-
stones or collapse beneath them in weak timbers
over a well. Hay balers didn't care what they baled,
and silage choppers didn't care what they chopped.
But mostly the danger the boys knew was in stories
about what happened somewhere, someplace, just
out of sight, in the next county, down the road six
miles, somewhere else. The bull that crushed a man
against a gate. The woman who drowned trying to
save her child from rushing spring floods. The man
who broke his neck falling from the haymow. The
tornado that killed a whole family except the two-
month-old baby who was found in a lilac bush without a scratch on her.

The boys listened to the stories, and they didn't

argue with the truth of them. They'd had their own fair share of close calls. There was the eighty-pound hay bale that fell thirty feet and exploded in a green spray around them, and the lightning that splintered a huge boxelder tree right after they decided to run out from under that very tree and play in the rain. Once a steel splinter from the corn sheller fly-wheel whirred like a table saw past their heads. And they had their cuts and bruises. Knuckles that looked as if they'd been gnawed on by meat grinders. Sprained ankles and wrists. Blood blisters that took toenails and fingernails off as they healed. Small concussions that were good for week-long headaches. Wood slivers of all sizes that had punctured every part of their bodies. And that's not even counting all the skinned knees and nose bleeds. The boys had plenty of bangings-around, but nothing so bad that they weren't able to talk about it, maybe even boast about it, the next week.

In town on Saturday nights, the grown-ups would point out what terrible things had happened to other people:

See those farmers with all those missing fingers? Cornpickers did that.

See that boy who doesn't have an arm in his sleeve? Power take-off did that.

The evidence was everywhere: missing thises and missing thats. Hobblers and limpers and a scar-face or two. Farms tore lots of people up, no doubt about it.

Then the grown-ups would always come up with the clincher: That could have been you, they'd say. That could have been you.

Of course, it could have been them. The boys knew that. They also knew that it was impossible to explain that they still lived without fear, lived as if every day held the promise of adventures in the sunlight, even if the sky was dark, even if the icicles hanging from the eaves on the barns could drop at any moment like dazzling swords and impale them to the snow—the way one did to this twelve-year-old not so far away, just far enough away that the boys didn't know his name.

The Hornets' Nest

The leaves had fallen and with them a hornets' nest. The boys found pieces of the nest among the oak leaves. It was prettier than the leaves—like beautiful paper, but softer.

It looked like the hornets had put a little bit of everything into that nest. Somebody's blue sock chewed up and woven in with the yellow flower and red string. All those colors mixed through the color of dead oak leaves. The boys took the pieces out into the sunlight and touched them and studied them for a long time.

Then they tried to put them back together and did pretty well. They made wallpaper glue and ground up some leaves to mix with the glue, and fit all the pieces together until it looked just like the hornets' nest. They tied what they had made back up in the tree with some string.

That was also the year the boys repaired their tree

house. They found some old shingles and a few two-by-fours nobody was using. They were a little careless putting their own house together, but it held. It was a good year for fixing houses.

The next spring the hornets would not be going back to their nest, but they would be hanging around the boys' tree house more than usual.

Garden Rabbits

There were the fuzzy sharp-toothed ones that nipped tender shoots of lettuce and cabbage before they could dream of the salad bowl, the kind that multiplied as quickly as aphids and were as hard to discourage from their nibbling ways. But there was another kind of garden rabbit. These too were fruitful and multiplied in great abundance, though they did not hop. They were zucchini.

The boys did not like to eat zucchini very much. The taste was as dull as potatoes without salt or butter or sour cream, and the texture was slimy as cooked okra. But in August when the lettuce had bolted and the cabbage had died, when even most of the tomatoes had ripened and the wine-colored beets bulged from the earth ready for harvest, the zucchini caught a second breath: the yellow blossoms quickly turned into small green fingers that within a week were the size of cucumbers and in two weeks the size of small watermelons. Why couldn't the animal garden rabbits eat these vegetable garden rabbits instead of the carrots and lettuce?

If the boys didn't do something, they knew it would mean zucchini in eggs for breakfast, fried zucchini and onions for dinner, boiled zucchini for supper. Zucchini casseroles! Zucchini salads! Zucchini pie if there was a recipe for one hiding somewhere!

The oldest boy had a plan. Over supper, as they all swallowed the soggy chunks of zucchini, he said, We have so many zucchini, we should give some to the poor people who don't have anything to eat.

The oldest boy had never in his life suggested giving anything to anybody, not even to his friends. And now he was thinking of poor people he didn't even know?

The grown-ups thought it was a wonderful idea and even brought it up in their family devotions: *That the abundance of the earth should be given to all, they prayed. Yea, even to the neediest of our number.*

On Saturday night the boys loaded the car trunk with big zucchini before they went into town. The boys agreed that they would spend the evening giving the zucchini to poor people they met.

Look at them, said one of the grown-ups, as the

boys loaded their arms with zucchini and started down the streets looking for poor people. Aren't they wonderful?

The boys couldn't really tell a poor person from a rich person, so they started offering zucchini to everyone they met. They figured the rich people wouldn't take them and the poor people would. But it seemed that poor people were few and far between when it came to feeding them zucchini.

When the boys got to the big parking lot next to a Wal★Mart that had just replaced most of the stores downtown, the oldest boy said, Let's just put some in the back seat of everybody's car. We might not be getting them to the poor people, but at least we're still giving them away.

This is what they did and within a half hour they were rid of all the zucchini. The grown-ups thought the boys' charity had been so successful that they let the boys load up the trunk of the car with zucchini the next Saturday night too.

The boys went straight to the Wal★Mart parking lot. But word had gotten out that if you didn't lock your car doors somebody would fill the back seat of your car with giant zucchini.

Oh no, said the oldest boy, after they had tried all the car doors in the parking lot. We're stuck with them. We'll be eating zucchini until Christmas!

Then one of the boys pretended to drop one on the street as he crossed on the way back toward their car. The other boys followed suit, dropping zucchini, one after another. Whoops, whoops, whoops, as the zucchini dropped to the street.

The boys stood on the sidewalk and watched the cars pass by, some of them slowing down and swerving to miss the shattered vegetables. But in a few minutes the zucchini had been mushed up and the cars didn't even slow down. And that was how the last of the green garden rabbits died. Smeared out on the street like so much road-kill.

The Stray Cat in the Garden

A stray cat was hiding in the garden and the boys were supposed to shoo him away without stepping on any of the tomatoes.

The boys weren't interested in shooing the stray cat away. They wanted to catch him. It would be like catching a wild tiger in the jungle. Better than that, it would be like capturing a terrorist that didn't even speak ordinary cat language. They didn't talk about what they'd do with the cat if they did capture him. They could decide that later when they had the cat at their mercy.

The stray cat was a cool one, neither skittery nor afraid. His black and white colors stood out among the tomatoes and his gold eyes followed them curiously as they circled in around him. Maybe he was sick. Maybe he had rabies. No doubt about it, no matter what act this cat was putting on, he was dangerous.

Capturing him without being injured themselves would make them super heroes.

We need sacks to keep from getting scratched, said the oldest boy.

And a strong wooden box to hold him, said the youngest.

The boys got their capturing equipment together: thick feed sacks and a wooden crate with a top that could be nailed down as soon as they had this wild or crazy or sick stray cat in captivity.

They inched closer, from different directions.

Stare into his eyes, said the oldest boy. We'll hypnotize him.

The wild and scary stray cat watched them coming. He wasn't moving. He was holding his ground. If the hypnotizing was working, the cat wasn't giving any signals, one way or another.

It seemed to take forever, they moved so slowly, putting their feet down gradually with each step, walking as if they were walking on eggs. Walking so carefully that they weren't squashing any tomatoes or scaring the wild cat, all the while keeping their wide eyes on the yellow cat eyes, which had sharp black stripes down the centers, pupils shaped like daggers.

The boys kept edging closer. The cat kept on not moving. Nothing kept happening.

And then they were there. No more than a foot away from the crazy stray cat. Close enough to reach down and touch him. Close enough to smother him with feed sacks and haul him screeching and scratching into the wooden box where they'd slam the lid down and nail it tight and let the critter howl for mercy.

Then the cat moved. He stood up and arched his back.

Get ready! said the oldest boy in a loud whisper.

But the stray cat wasn't getting up to run or fight. He was arching his back like a normal cat getting up from a nap. The stray cat yawned.

Look how skinny he is, said the youngest boy.

One boy lowered a corner of a sack. The stray cat lifted his head toward the sack, as if he wanted to be petted.

The boy lay the sack down, and touched the head of the wild and crazy stray cat, which immediately started purring. The cat lay down on his back and opened his legs.

He wants his tummy rubbed, said another boy.

I can see that, said the oldest boy.

All the boys' hands reached for the stray cat, stroking the black and white fur, rubbing the ears and neck. Then the cat licked one of the boy's hands. And kept licking, until he had all of the boys at his mercy. Their only worry now was how to hide the stray cat in the barn and sneak him food and milk without the grown-ups seeing what they were up to.

Who Had Six Toes

One of the girls at school had six toes on one foot.

Did you hear about Maggie's toes? asked one girl who didn't like her.

What? said one of the boys. And that was it for Maggie. Soon everyone at school knew she had six toes on one foot. At first they just watched her as she walked, trying to figure out which foot had all those toes.

Then they teased her. Hey, Maggie, what are you hiding in your shoe? one boy asked.

Six toes, said Maggie. Want to see them?

Yes! shouted everyone, not teasing anymore.

First, I should tell you, said Maggie. It is a magic toe.

The boys started to snicker.

It can give you a toothache. Or an earache. It can make you cross-eyed. It will give you diarrhea if it wants to.

Nobody snickered anymore because Maggie got all A's in school and probably knew what she was saying.

Will it hurt us if we look at it? said one of the boys.

Maybe not, said Maggie.

Maggie took off her shoe and then her sock. It was the left foot. Most of the boys had guessed wrong. And there sat the extra toe on Maggie's little white foot. It was smaller than the others and sat piggy-back between the second and third toes.

Can you wiggle it? asked one of the boys in a whisper.

If I want to, said Maggie.

Do you want to? he whispered again, with much respect.

Yes, said Maggie. And she wiggled her magic toe.

Just then, the girl who had told everyone about Maggie's extra toe ran away crying and holding her hands over her ears.

Kickers

Listen to me, said the boys' grandfather. When I was a boy, you had to be smart or you could get hurt.

Their grandfather had already sat down in his old swivel chair. He lit one of his cigars and took a big puff. The boys made themselves comfortable on the floor.

We milked by hand in those days, he said. And you had to look out for kickers. It was hard to tell which heifer was a kicker until you tried to milk her. Kicking seemed like an instinct to some of them, but some of them got better with practice. And just like with a good bucking bronco, you couldn't predict a good kicker's moves.

He laid his cigar down and rubbed his hands together. You had your four types of kickers, he said. There was your side-winder kicker who'd catch you in the stomach. You have to think of a hind leg going up about two feet and then making a U-turn out to the side at about forty miles an hour.

He made a quick swing of his arm. That's your side-winder, he said.

Then you had your jack-hammer kicker. She'd lift a leg straight up and come down with it straight in the bucket you had under her.

Sort of like your jack-hammer kicker was your pogo-stick kicker. She liked to bounce on her rear legs and could just as easy break your jaw with her hip as smash your foot with her hoofs. Main difference between your jack-hammer and your pogo-stick was that the jack-hammer kicker tried to give you a knock-out punch and the pogo-stick kicker tried to get you with quick jabs.

But then you had your fourth kind of kicker. Here's where you get your art and finesse. The bumble-bee kicker. Maybe you could spot a young heifer as a bumble-bee kicker type, but it usually took her three or four years to perfect her style. The bumble-bee kicker's hoof would come up a little off the straw and sort of hang there. Then it would start jittering and bouncing around in the air like it was looking for a target. All of a sudden, Blam! Maybe she'd go for the bucket. Maybe for your wrist. Sometimes she'd take out somebody who was standing behind her. You never knew for sure. Whatever it was she went for, she'd hit it, and it had a real sting!

Wow! said the oldest boy. How'd you learn to keep from getting kicked?

The grandfather relit his cigar.

Now that's another story, he said. You had your factory-made shackles you could hook on the legs of the easy ones. There was rope that you could tie in different ways around the rear legs. Or you could tie a rope tight around the middle. This was supposed to paralyze the rear legs a little bit. Then there was kindness. You don't like to tell too many people about this method because they'll think you're a softy. But I always gave kindness a try. I'd pet and feed a kicker until she trusted me.

Did kindness always work? asked the youngest boy.

Their grandfather looked toward the window, as if he could read all of his memories out there. I'm afraid not, he said. A real kicker just made a profession of it. Kicking is the only thing that interested her and she made no secret of it. That's why milking was so dangerous when I was a boy.

I've never been kicked by a cow, said the youngest boy.

No, no, said the grandfather. And you probably won't either.

Because I am nice to them? he asked.

No, no, said the grandfather. Because kicking has been bred out of them. You hardly have to keep your guard up at all any more when you're around cows.

That's good, isn't it? said the youngest boy.

What do you think? said the grandfather.

The Corn Bin

The shelled corn bin was like a huge box over the alleyway of the corn crib. Millions of crisp and yellow corn kernels, ten feet deep, and ten feet square at the top. The boys liked to dive into it, letting it sting their hands and faces as they squirmed until they almost disappeared into the golden wonder of it all.

Sometimes they pretended it was quicksand, swaying back and forth in it as they slowly sank down to their armpits, and another one of them would fling them a rope in this great but pretend rescue mission.

None of this was dangerous. But the boys were told not to play in the shelled corn bin when it was being emptied. You could get sucked down in a whirlpool of shelled corn. You could get buried in corn so far that you wouldn't be able to get out. You could choke. You could drown in corn is what could happen. You'd be four feet under the corn before the corn chute would be stopped when a wagon under the grain bin was full.

Then what? Nobody would know what happened to you. If a boy disappeared, people always looked in the wells and cisterns first to see if he had fallen in. But who would think of looking for a boy in the middle of a big corn bin? It might be months before anybody found you. And then you'd probably be half eaten by rats.

The youngest boy knew that the problem with doing something you're not supposed to do when the other boys were around was that one of them would always tell—and blame him. They'd say that it was the youngest boy's idea. It's not our fault, they'd say. We tried to stop him, they'd say.

So the youngest boy waited until none of the other boys were watching to go play in the shelled corn bin while it was being emptied into a large wagon beneath it in the corn crib alley.

At first the moving grain was like a golden funnel forming before his eyes, and the small cave-in at the middle was like the center of the flour in a sifter as it slowly indented, or the way the center of a milk shake caves in if you have the straw in the middle. Then he saw the corn start to swirl a little. This is where the grown-ups got that whirlpool idea. But it was no fun if you couldn't feel the kernels of corn moving against your body. There was no way a person could drown in shelled corn, he knew that. It was just another one of those things grown-ups said to keep kids scared. So the youngest boy jumped into the middle of the whirlpool of shelled corn. It was great. It was like having somebody rubbing you softly with a back-scratcher all over your body. Gently scratching you and turning you over at the same time. He lay back and moved his arms the way he would if he were trying to swim on his back. The moving and gently swirling yellow corn was a million little fingers moving across his body, making every inch of him tingle.

Then something grabbed both of his feet from the bottom and started pulling. He thought of the time he hooked a big mud turtle on his fishing line and slowly dragged the stubborn weight to shore. Now he was the mud turtle and something was pulling him. He tried moving his legs the way he would if he were running, but the suction from the opening at the bottom of the corn bin was pulling him down. His hands were still free and he beat at the corn with them, but all of the kernels were working together now, working against him, working to pull him down under. At first it was the corn dust in his nostrils and eyes, and then the sting of the kernels on his face. He tried to take a deep breath. And couldn't.

It was as if his body exploded then and light came back as quickly as it had gone out. He pushed corn away from his face and rolled with the swirl of the corn, cupping corn in his hands and pulling toward the light, turning over and over the way a log might turn over on the surface of water, but with his arms moving all the while, beating at the corn as he pulled himself against the suction. And then the sucking stopped.

He crawled out of the half-empty corn bin and looked down at what he had conquered.

I'm not four feet under the corn, choked, dead and drowned, he said to himself. That wasn't so bad, he said to himself. I could do that again if I wanted to.

He stood up, but the feeling of pride burst as quickly as it had come. He couldn't tell the grown-ups about his accomplishment without being punished, and without a witness his friends who wouldn't punish him would never believe him.

The Boys Go to Ask
a Neighbor for Some Apples

When the boys went to one neighbor's farm to ask him if they might pick some of his apples, they could not find him anywhere. They went into the house, and then to all the buildings and called for him. They checked the machine shed to see if the tractor was out. It wasn't.

They started looking behind things—behind the pig troughs and cattle feeders, behind the fences and wagons. Finally, when they crawled over some hay bales in the barn—in a very dark corner of the barn—they saw him. He was praying to his animals.

On his knees with his hands crossed on his lap. Praying to a piglet, a dog, a cat, and a bull calf. He had fed each of them its own kind of food, so they were quiet as he prayed.

He was saying, Little animals with four feet on the ground, teach the rocks to lie in their places, tell the oceans never to rise and the mountains never to fall. Little ones, give your gentle ways to me.

The boys slipped away and went to wait in the yard. When the man came out of the barn, they asked him about apples. He brought a large basket and said they could fill it with the ripest and largest apples from his trees. Not only that. He said they could keep the basket to carry feed to their animals.

An Alligator in the Sandpit

No one believed it when it came out in the newspaper that an alligator had been seen in the sandpit.

But sure as can be everybody started watching for it, sitting in the cornfields around the sandpit and waiting for that alligator to show itself. Nobody brought guns. That would come later. When somebody really saw the alligator—some place besides the newspaper.

The boys were not allowed out there at night—but on Saturdays, in the daylight, it was all right. And they liked it. It was like fishing, only with your eyes. Sitting there and waiting for a nibble. Waiting for the alligator to make a ripple on the surface like a bobber to tell them it was really there.

Do you think anybody saw that alligator? No. Nobody saw it. Not even the boys with their good eyes. Did the newspaper just make that up to be funny? Who knows.

The farmer out there complained that his corn was getting flattened where everybody sat and watched for the alligator. Maybe the alligator died from fright seeing all those people on the shore. Maybe the turtles ate it then.

But everybody got to talking to each other while they watched. It was like they were sitting around a big bonfire. Nobody looked at each other, just at the water as far down as they could see. Pretty soon somebody started singing and then everybody was singing—even on Saturday afternoon when the boys were there. They blushed a little and held hands with people.

This lasted until corn picking time when there was too much to do.

Who Are Those People Anyhow?

At first the boys didn't get it. What it was that made the grown-ups talk so much about this one farmer and his family. They seemed to get their corn planted at the same time as everybody else. Their alfalfa fields were just as green and their oat fields just as yellow.

But then the boys started noticing what the grown-ups noticed. That other farmer had a DeLaval milking machine instead of a Surge. He drove a Studebaker instead of a Ford. He planted Pioneer seed corn instead of Dekalb. He had an Oliver tractor instead of a John Deere. He planted spruce trees in his grove instead of ash. His buildings were tan instead of red. You'd see Guernsey cows in his pasture instead of Holsteins, and Rhode Island Reds in his chicken coop instead of Leghorns—and the empty feed sacks lying against one of the sheds said Purina instead of Felco. Even his hog yards looked suspicious, what with all those spotted Poland Chinas and not one Duroc or Chester White.

At first it was enough to make the boys curious, but after a while they started to wonder too. Just who are those people anyhow? Even the name on their mailbox had a fishy look and sound to it. On Saturday nights when this farmer's kids showed up in town like everybody else, the boys stayed away from them, but they knew they'd better be ready to fight if it came to that.

Moley

On Saturdays when the boys went into town they liked to watch the dwarf shoe repairman named Moley sit on his high stool tapping nails. It was best to watch him before lunch, before he went to the tavern where he drank a lot of beer and ran around the pool table with a little stool to stand on when he shot.

When Moley drank too much beer too many weeks in a row, people got angry with him and didn't bring him their shoes anymore. You could tell how much beer he was drinking by seeing how bad people's shoes looked on the street.

Then one day Moley quit drinking beer. This was after many weeks of the boys' going to watch him tapping nails but not finding him in his shop.

When Moley quit drinking beer, he wanted everyone to know about it. So he started drinking half-gallon cans of tomato and grapefruit juice and stacking the empty cans in his little shop. When people stopped by his shop now, he counted the juice cans for them and they were supposed to know from this how much beer he wasn't drinking.

Ninety-nine cans last count! people said on the street—and soon everyone brought their shoes.

Those were good Saturdays for the boys. They could go to Moley's shop at any time of the day and see his little hands go down inside a shoe to find its problem. Sometimes, to show they liked him, the boys helped stack the cans in tens to make the counting easier.

But one Saturday, in the middle of the corn harvesting, after Moley's shop had gotten so full of juice cans that you could hardly get inside, the boys came to his shop door and it was locked. Through the windows they saw that all the juice cans were gone.

Of course, Moley had taken to beer again and had cleaned out the juice cans to make no secret of it. Still he had built up enough good will during those juice days that his shelves were packed with shoes that needed him—credit enough waiting there for months of good times in the tavern.

The Pet Squirrel

FOR SUSAN WILLIAMS

The boys started sneaking kernels of corn out on the back porch for the squirrels. One of the squirrels got very tame. It ran up within a few feet of the boys when they threw corn out to it. After a while, it ate right from their hands.

That's when they told the grown-ups about the squirrel, now that it would be too late for them to say it was foolish wasting corn on a squirrel that would never want to be a pet anyhow.

Then the squirrel started sitting on the kitchen window sill. And came in the house when the window was open.

The pet squirrel moved in and made itself at home.

Almost all the time you might see it sitting on the back of a chair, listening to the radio, or in the kitchen drinking from the sink.

One day, the youngest boy yelled, Who put nuts in my coat pockets?

The other boys checked their coat pockets too. The pockets were full of nuts.

A few days later, the old kitchen radio sounded strange. The boys found nuts packed in the back between the tubes. The squirrel was reminding everyone to get ready for winter.

So the boys checked their mittens to make sure they didn't have any holes in them. And their overshoes to make sure they didn't leak. The squirrel kept busy stuffing nuts into everything.

What a smart squirrel, said one of the boys.

Then, just before Halloween, the boys found the pet squirrel dead on the kitchen floor. What had happened was it had gotten up in the cupboard and tried to get into a box of Wheaties. It didn't know the box would topple when it got all its weight on the top. The fall didn't kill the squirrel, but the sharp corner of the box came down on the squirrel's head as they hit the floor together. The boys found a little dent above its eye. The squirrel was covered with Wheaties.

So, in the cold fall air, the boys carried the squirrel to the garden to bury it.

Look, said one of the boys, pointing into the trees. The other squirrels were watching.

There sat the other squirrels, their tails twitching nervously where they sat on the bare branches.

Maybe this squirrel wasn't so smart after all, said one of the boys, shoveling dirt over it.

In Which the Librarian
Writes a Letter to the Editor

There weren't many outdoor privies left. Ones that didn't rot from age were tipped over on Halloween nights by mischievous boys. And the owners of the few that did remain did everything they could to outsmart the boys who were trying to figure out ways to tip them over.

One very mean farmer looked out for his privy with a big machete that he flashed around town on Halloween day.

I'm going to wait inside my privy with this thing, he said, and chop up anyone who comes near it.

Some older boys fixed him by taking a long rope and running with five boys on either end until the rope came across the rear of the privy. Keeping their distance this way, they tipped the privy onto its front door before the man with the machete even heard them coming. The only way he could get out was through the seat holes, which meant falling into the stinky pit.

The toilet-tippers didn't always get the last laugh. One clever farmer moved his privy ahead six feet so that when the boys came up behind to tip it on Halloween night, they were the ones who fell into the stinky pit.

There were so many tricks that privy owners and boys played on each other that a book could be written about it.

But the only person who wrote anything about it in those parts was the town librarian. She was one of these people who always look angry, but she usually didn't say what she was thinking. She wrote a letter to the editor which was printed in the newspaper. She said it was terrible the fuss people made over outhouses on Halloween. She was bothered, she wrote, by the scatological obsession of our youth. That's what she wrote in the paper: *scatological obsession of our youth*!

Most people didn't understand her letter, but the boys figured out that she didn't like what they did to outhouses on Halloween nights.

Too bad for the librarian, she had an outhouse too.

And hers was not old and rotting. Hers was quite new and the only toilet she had. She lived a simple life of order and neatness. Her outhouse was so neat and clean that many people didn't even know it was her toilet.

But the boys did. And what she wrote in the newspaper gave them an idea. They started with forty squares of active yeast. They shoved these down into the librarian's toilet with broom handles while she was busy reshelving books in the library. And like the world's biggest loaf of bread, the toilet contents did begin to rise. And rise. First the bulging mass came up through the toilet seat holes, then lifted the neat little shanty into the air. The yeast kept working until some people said the raised privy looked like a steeple on top of that big mound. Others said it looked like a witch's hat on top of a very ugly witch's head.

The newspaper printed a picture and a caption which read: *Local librarian discovers scatology on the rise, as shown in this backyard photograph.*

The Man Who Raised Turkeys

The boys wondered about this one farmer down the road who did nothing on his little farm but raise turkeys. He said if you really cared about one thing, that should be enough for everybody. He said he knew more about turkeys than any other person in the whole wide world.

Just look at them, he'd say. They know I'm their best friend. You ever see such happy turkeys?

The boys looked hard at the turkeys. They did look happy, eating away at the little cup-shaped troughs the man had built for them. The turkeys even gobbled in a happy way, sounding like grown-ups bragging to each other about how nice their kids' projects looked at the 4-H fair.

But as Thanksgiving Day got closer, the boys found the turkey man harder and harder to figure out. He was out there with his turkeys all the time, feeding them from his hand and talking as if to the dearest creatures alive. Didn't he care that Thanksgiving was the end of the line?

Look, he said. Look how eager they're getting. They can tell it's almost Thanksgiving.

He reached down and stroked the shiny white wing feathers of the biggest bird. You know, don't you? my clever little friend.

Clever little friend? said one of the boys.

They knew better than to call turkeys clever. Friendly, maybe. Maybe even obedient. But clever? Hardly. The boys knew turkeys didn't have enough sense to put their heads down in a rainstorm to keep rain from filling the nostrils that sat on top of their beaks like little rain gauges. Turkey nostrils would fill up and they'd drown if it rained more than an inch an hour. Turkeys were too stupid to get out of the rain. Maybe they and the turkey man were meant for each other.

The week before Thanksgiving, the boys went back for one last look at how things were going to go during the turkeys' last days some place other than people's dinner platters.

The man was still there, feeding and petting them. Then one of the boys just out and said, If those turkeys had a brain in their heads, they'd peck your hand off.

This didn't bother the turkey man at all. Oh, no, he said. My turkeys know what's coming. They know what they're on earth for. It's almost their special day, and they're ready. Watch this.

He had brought the chopping block into the turkey pen. His ax sat right next to it. Watch this, he said.

He took one of the turkeys and laid it on the chopping block. He held it down with one hand, and with the other raised the ax.

I'm not going to do it now, he said, but watch.

As the man raised the ax, the turkey bent its neck back, like a man lifting his chin to make it easier to shave his neck.

Look, he said, see how this big tom leans his neck back for the ax. He's ready for Thanksgiving.

The boys left. Nonsense never came any thicker than that. At least now they knew the turkey man was just as stupid as the turkeys.

One boy said, I bet he really believes it, that the turkey put his head back like that to make it easier to kill him.

Yeah, said another. The dummy.

They didn't have to say any more. They knew about

animals. They knew what rabbits meant when they put their ears down and froze in place. They knew what a dog was doing when it lay on its back and opened its legs to its attacker. That turkey wasn't giving anybody permission for anything. That turkey was begging for mercy. The boys weren't going to go back and visit the turkey farm again before Thanksgiving, they knew that. But what to think of the turkey man and all his stupid turkeys? Maybe they did deserve each other. That's the best the boys could say for them.

2

If the Weather Stayed Nice

Isn't it wonderful the way the ducks fly south for winter! exclaimed an old woman who always saw the best side of nature.

What's so wonderful about it? asked Uncle Jack. If the weather stayed nice, they wouldn't have to go through all that trouble flying south.

The old woman ruffled her shawl. If the weather stayed nice, she said in a mocking voice. If the weather stayed nice! Don't you know that flying south makes the ducks strong and healthy?

Flying south keeps them from getting their tails frozen in the ice is what it does, said Uncle Jack. If the weather stayed nice, the ducks could spend their time swimming in the quiet ponds. Or preening themselves. Or learning how to sing. Instead of their miserable quacking, maybe they'd sit and listen to themselves and learn how to carry a tune.

Carry a tune! shouted the old woman, fluttering a

little. Quacking is their own beautiful music! She waddled toward Uncle Jack, and she might have attacked him if it had not been for a cold November breeze that caught the back of her neck. It stunned her old body and brought out a horrendous sneeze. She looked behind her to see the huge black cloud that was rolling in from the north. She tried flapping her flabby arms, but her old body stood there quivering.

Is Uncle Jack Crazy?

The boys didn't really know all that much about Uncle Jack. They knew he lived in a tiny white house on a small acreage close to town. They knew he made a living by building small and useless things like little windmills and wishing wells that people bought and put on their front lawns. Other than that, they didn't know what made him tick. He dressed in old blue overalls and wore a straw hat. In the winter time, he still wore his straw hat but put fuzzy green ear muffs under it to keep his big ears warm. He was always smiling, it seemed, and he walked funny. That's about all they knew.

But it was always fun when they'd see him on the streets in town on Saturday nights. Some people would try to tease him because he seemed so different, but you couldn't really make fun of Uncle Jack because he was always ready with a strange or tricky answer. Maybe somebody would say, Hey, Uncle Jack, sold any of your wishing wells lately? And he would quickly answer with something like, Well, when I wish to sell a wishing well, I wish you well my wells to wish. That kind of talk made people scratch their heads, and then buy one of his wishing wells.

Is Uncle Jack Crazy? asked the youngest boy.

Probably, said the oldest boy. Probably. Why don't you ask him?

But, like everybody else, the youngest boy had heard just enough of Uncle Jack's talk to leave well enough alone.

The Rich Man

One farmer got rich when his father died. One day he had one farm and the next day he had four. His older sister died in a car crash a year ago and both of his younger brothers had drowned in a flood the year before that.

He should have known all those farms would be coming to him, the only child left, but he was not ready for it, and now that he had it all he didn't know how to act. Couldn't look people in the face, yet couldn't help puffing up a little when the bankers sent presents and promises. Couldn't help pulling up to the implement dealer and looking at new tractors the day after his father's funeral, yet drove away quickly when people saw him drooling over that shining new machinery. And in a few weeks, after the spending on all his good credit started, couldn't help biting his lip nervously when a neighbor lady said, So sorry to hear about your father's passing—and so soon after your poor sister's tragic death. Let us know if you need anything.

If he needs anything, he can sell one of his father's farms, someone said behind his back.

The boys didn't know what to make of all this talk. They even heard somebody say the man didn't deserve all of those farms because some were meant for his dead brothers and sister. He should give the farms to charity for a memorial, someone said. That would be the decent thing to do.

People said being rich was making the man too big for his britches. He had more stars than tears in his eyes, that's for sure, they said.

To the boys, it looked more like the man had more fear in his eyes than either tears or stars. And he didn't look like he was too big for his britches, he looked like his britches were to big for him the way he kept tripping on them trying to get from one farm to the next. He did get the new tractors, all right, but what did people expect, what with four farms to take care of by himself?

An Unexpected Blizzard

One winter night a blizzard came when no one was expecting it. Some pregnant sows that were not penned up got caught in that blizzard. A few knew it was time to come in and were safe in the hog house the next morning, but most of the sows stayed out in the blizzard and disappeared under the snowdrifts.

The boys went out as soon as they heard there would be no school and started helping find the buried sows. They were lighter than the men, so they walked over the snowbanks without sinking down. They used sticks to poke through the snow, and could tell when they hit a sow—it moved! Sometimes making the stick jump right back out of the snow!

Here's one! one of the boys would call. The men would come with big feed scoops to dig the sow out and get her safe into the hog house.

Pretty soon the boys had found all the buried sows. Except one. There was one sow missing.

They went back with their sticks, poking every-where in the pig lot where the sow might be lying. The men helped. Everyone poking in the snowbanks for the lost sow. After several hours, they guessed that the sow must be dead and that even if they were poking her, she wasn't moving.

The boys sat up late that night, feeling bad that they had not found the lost sow. The next morning there was more snow, so all the boot tracks and stick marks were covered up. The boys had to give up, but they still thought about that sow.

Three weeks later there was a big thaw. The boys watched for the body of the lost sow to start showing through the snow. They couldn't figure out what spot they could have missed with their sticks, poking.

At noon one Saturday, the lost sow stood up, broke through the dirty melting snow and stood there wob-bling. And she had little pigs! Six of them still alive, and though the sow was skinny the little pigs were fine—tugging at her dugs as she tried to walk away.

The men put fresh straw in a pen they prepared just for this sow. They even hung a heat lamp over the spot where she would be lying. The boys carried the little pigs to the house and put them in a box by the stove to get them warm and feed them milk from a bottle before bringing them back to the sow where she was getting ready for them in her warm nest.

What happens to animals that are so lucky like this? one boy asked.

I don't know, said another.

The boys watched these pigs grow up. They were little miracles to the boys, but pretty soon they hardly looked any different from the other pigs. When they were big enough, they were sent to market with all those other ordinary pigs. And somebody somewhere was eating that special meat, and not even knowing it.

The Albino Fox

Everyone had seen the albino fox a time or two. Especially in winter when, instead of hiding against the snow, it lay on clear spots on the dark plowed fields and basked in the sun.

What would a patch of white snow be doing on the side of a plowed hill where all the rest of the snow had melted?

Someone would get out his binoculars and, sure enough, it would be the albino fox.

You couldn't find anyone who didn't want to shoot that albino fox and stuff it for a trophy. But nobody could get close enough for a good shot. It always got up in time and ran for the snow where it disappeared like a drift in the wind.

I want to get those pink eyes in my sights, said one farmer who had been hunting the albino fox for years. So he got three greyhound dogs from the race track and a big scope for his rifle.

The neighbors came to look at his dogs and rifle scope and wondered if he could really do it. Everyone said they would telephone him if they saw the fox.

Nobody's going to get that tricky white fox. That white fox is too clever, they said.

The next time someone saw the albino fox, they telephoned the man with the dogs. And the neighbors followed him in their cars as he drove off in his pickup with the greyhounds and new scope.

He let the dogs out on one side of the hill and went to wait on the other side—a half mile from where the albino fox was basking in the sun on the plowed field.

The dogs got the scent of the fox right away and caught up with it in no time at all. The fox looked like a cripple when those fast dogs were after it. The dogs played with the albino fox, throwing it in the air and letting it run a little ways before catching it again. That fox was so mixed up that it ran toward the man with the big scope. Pretty soon the fox and dogs were so close that the man called off his dogs. The fox sat in the snow panting and the man found its pink eyes in his new scope.

That sure was easy, said one farmer who was watching.

Ever try shooting the broad side of a barn from the inside? teased another farmer.

I'll bet you'd have good luck hunting sheep with those dogs, said another.

The man who shot the albino fox felt so foolish that he hid his trophy in the cellar. But it was too late. He could just as well have kept it in his living room because nobody came to visit him anymore anyhow.

A New Year's Story

The boys watched and listened to the bad year push its way through the months. Spring came too slow and summer went too fast. And then that early frost in September! It was as if weather was the kind of bully who'd push you over the cliff after you were already falling.

Look at the corn, one grown-up said. What didn't shrivel from the early drought got drowned by the late flood.

The boys could see how bad it was. Cattle that coughed up feedlot dust one week were stuck knee-deep in mud holes the next. The only good thing all summer was when the dry-grass fire of August smacked into the flash-flood of September. They deserved each other.

When the ash settled and the mud dried, the boys figured the only thing they could hope for was a good Halloween. But the pumpkins were the size of softballs, and their jack-o-lanterns wouldn't hold anything bigger than one of those little birthday candles. It looked as if even kids couldn't get away from the meanness of this bad year.

We're skunked, said one grown-up.

The whole year's a dead duck, said another.

So what would people do when Thanksgiving came around? No way there'd be store-bought turkey this year, probably not even cranberries that in good times got shipped in from one of those rich and lucky places. Maybe it wouldn't have been so bad if the livestock had done any better than the crops. A couple of fat chickens or a big juicy ham wouldn't make their Thanksgiving table look anything like the Thanksgiving dinners they saw in magazines, the boys knew that. No way they'd have all those beautiful oranges and yellows with a big brown turkey in the middle, but a couple roasted chickens and a big pink ham—that would be something. But the weird weather gave the chickens such a bad case of lice that their feathers fell out, and they looked like they'd been picked off the road after a couple semis ran over them. The ham didn't look too good either, since all the fat pigs were sold to make up for the rotten crops, and the only pig left over was a runt that wasn't worth trucking to market.

Christmas wasn't any better, but then when New Year's got closer, somebody got the idea that everybody should make the best of a bad year. Since none of the families in their neighborhood had a good Thanksgiving or Christmas, nobody should eat New Year's dinner alone. They'd all get together so everybody could have a little bit of everybody else's little bit.

That's what happened. There were a couple buckets of Kool-aid for the kids and a couple gallons of coffee for the grown-ups, so everybody could drink themselves half full before sitting down for dinner. Every family brought heaping bowls of the bad year's leftovers. When the eating started, people chewed slow and talked a lot between bites. They didn't talk about money or building new barns. They didn't talk about new machinery or how many pounds the steers didn't gain in December. They talked about how the kids were doing in geography and spelling. Then someone told a joke about the weather.

Remember that real scorcher of a week last summer? one man asked. It was so hot and dry that this farmer fainted while he was fixing fence and it took a whole bucket of dust just to wake him up!

That was a good one, and everybody laughed over their half-empty plates.

Reminds me, said another, of that awful wind we had in September. I was digging post holes, and every time I got one dug the wind started blowing so hard it blew that hole right out of the ground and I had to start over.

The boys thought that was even funnier. One of them tipped his cup upside down to show what it would look like to have the wind blow a hole out of the ground.

Then a woman at the table said, That's nothing. You hear about this lady who was so bad-off she had to use rotten eggs to bake a Christmas cake? You, know, the really stinky kind that float when you put them in water. Well, that cake smelled so bad, the only thing her kids would eat was meat and potatoes!

She was telling this joke as she got ready to serve tiny slices of pumpkin pie, and that made everybody laugh even harder.

It wasn't long before the boys were rubbing their stomachs. They weren't sure if it was because they didn't have enough food or because they'd had too much. Or maybe they lost their appetite when the woman told her awful rotten-egg joke, or maybe their stomachs ached from laughing too hard. They weren't even sure any more what it was that had made the past year so bad, or what it would take to turn this new year into a good one.

Somebody at the table probably knew a joke about what happened to the person who thought things were bound to get better, but right now everybody was too busy laughing at the last joke to think of another one.

Boys' Work

There is snow, and then there is snow. There already had been snow enough for snowmen and snow forts, enough for fox-and-geese paths and snowball fights. But then came the real snowstorm, the one that had roamed around Canada for a while before deciding to come south for a celebration. The granddaddy snow-storm. Now there was enough snow and wind to make banks so high around the house that it looked like a sinking ship in a sea of frozen white waves. It was the kind of snowstorm that made snowmen and snow forts sound silly, the kind that made grown-ups say things like, It's really happened, Worse than thirty-six or Things will never be the same. It was the kind of snowstorm that meant one thing. It meant work. Boys' work.

The boys jumped out of an upstairs window with pots and pans and the one shovel that was kept in the house. Their job was to use these to dig a path back to the front door so that it would open. They landed waist-deep in the shallowest snow, and dug. Dug as if they were going to die out there if they didn't reach the door quickly, or as if the grown-ups would die inside the house if they weren't dug out soon. Hurry! they kept yelling to each other, but it didn't look as if they were all that interested in reaching the house. They were too busy showing the snow who was boss, chipping and chopping into its huge mass, flinging chunks of it high into the air, making the passage higher and higher and wider and wider.

When finally they found themselves getting hungry, they dug straight for the front door and had it cleared within a few minutes.

By the time the grown-ups opened the front door, it was as if a huge snowplow had been working around the house, mounding the snow ten feet high, making the path thirty feet wide.

The boys were rewarded inside with hot chocolate. They kept congratulating each other through the slurps, and the grown-ups added to the praise.

Then came these awful words: Now that we can get outside, we'd better go do the chores. Whose turn is it to get the eggs? Whose turn is it to feed the pigs? And who's going to clean the gutter before we milk the cows?

What? shouted the boys. We can't go out and do chores in this kind of weather!

Who Were Poor and Crazy

There was a family of poor and crazy people who lived in a house close to the railroad track. They were a father, a mother, and a little girl. When they were in town, they let their mouths hang open as if they were too tired to keep them closed. You could always see their tongues. They had big tongues.

In the summer they'd go to all the softball games. They'd go to the Fireman's Ball, the county fairs, the circus, and the Fourth of July picnic in the park. They'd hitch-hike to all the celebrations, and people always picked them up because they were poor and crazy.

But in the winter time the whole family always stayed home. When there was a blizzard, neighbors went over there with food to make sure they didn't starve.

One morning after a snowstorm the boys went along to bring food to these poor and crazy people. The car had to follow the snowplow to get there that day. The grown-ups wanted to teach the boys to be kind to people who needed help, so they let the boys push the baskets of food over the snowdrifts.

A screen porch leaned from the front of the house. When the boys got the basket of food up onto it, they slipped on the ice on the porch floor. Water hadn't made that ice. It was urine. Urine had run across the porch floor when the chamber pot got full. The pot sat inside the porch next to the front door.

Nobody had emptied the pot in the cold weather and pretty soon it was too late even if they had wanted to. The pot was frozen down and everything inside it was frozen solid. So the family had just kept using it, and it got fuller and fuller with urine and dung— which kept freezing every time they used it. Now it was so full that a big mound had grown on top. A mound that went straight up to a point where the last person had used it.

The boys knocked on the door and waited for the poor and crazy people to come and get the food.

Say, said the oldest boy, pointing at the pot with its big mound, that would remind me of an ice cream cone if it wasn't so cold out here.

Stupid, said the youngest boy. If it wasn't so cold out here, it wouldn't be there.

Potato Soup

It was a cold Saturday in the middle of the winter when one old sow decided to have thirteen of the tiniest pigs the boys had ever seen. The pigs all looked like runts and were so weak they couldn't break their own umbilical cords when they tried walking toward their mother's paps.

The boys figured there was nothing they could do to make the little pigs' lives any worse, so they put them in a big metal grain basket with a few handfuls of straw in the bottom and carried the basket to the house. They put it next to a pot of potato soup that was on the stove for lunch.

Look at that, said one of the boys as the basket warmed up. Those little pigs are getting bigger.

Sure enough, the pigs did look like they were growing. It was as if the heat in the basket was blowing them up to their real size.

Look at the soup, said another boy. It's growing too.

The soup bubbled up closer and closer and closer to the edge of the pot, and the smell of its steam made the boys hungry. But the pigs were starting to steam too and to jump around in the basket, making a clattering racket against the metal with their little hooves.

Quick! shouted one of the boys. We can't eat with all that noise.

They ran out with the clattering basket and emptied it against the sleeping sow. Now the heated-up little pigs plunged into their mother's warm belly. The boys watched them fill up on their first warm meal, watched and watched as the little pigs punched and sucked until milk was running from the corners of their mouths. Watching the pigs made the boys hungrier than ever, and one of them yelled, The soup! We forgot about the soup! They got back to the house just in time to see that someone had already poured the hot soup into brimming bowls for each of them.

Winter Chores

When the boys complained about having to do chores on cold winter nights, their grandfather told them, You boys have it so easy nowadays. Let me tell you about the chores we had to do when I was a boy.

The boys sat back to listen.

You see, chores weren't finished when we got in the house. On very cold nights my brothers and I had two chores before going to sleep. We had to tie the blankets down to the bed frames so we wouldn't kick the covers off in our dreams and get frostbite on our hands and feet. And we had to empty the chamber pot so that what was in it wouldn't freeze and need thawing on the stove in the morning.

The boys watched their grandfather's face to see if he was smiling through this story. He wasn't. This probably was a true story. He went on:

One night we remembered to tie down the blankets but forgot to empty the pot. When we were all settled in, somebody remembered, but it was so cold that night that no one would get out of bed and go outside to empty it. Storm windows had already been put on so we couldn't even cheat by emptying it out the window.

Now the boys saw their grandfather smile a little. They giggled, but they were still pretty sure this was a true story, and they could tell it wasn't over yet.

So, their grandfather went on, we argued for a while about whose turn it was to empty the pot and then argued some more about who would have to thaw it out in the morning if nobody emptied it that night. I knew that if we kept arguing like that the pot would freeze before we even got to sleep. Then I got this idea. I said, Let's keep the pot under the blankets with us tonight—then it won't freeze. My brothers said, All right, but it will have to be in your bed. So I jumped out of bed and ran across that cold linoleum floor and got that pot. I had to loosen my blankets to get it under the covers with me.

Ugh, said the youngest boy. You really did this?

Sure did, said their grandfather. I put it right under my feet so I could keep it from tipping over in my bed.

Ugh, all the boys said together now.

So there I was, me and that half-full pot under the covers together. At first, the metal felt cold, but soon it warmed up with me and kept my feet warm. This made all the other boys jealous, and the next night they all wanted to take their turn with the pot in bed with them. Sometimes we even fought over who could have it in his bed.

Did you ever spill any of it? asked the youngest boy.

Of course not, said their grandfather. In those days boys were very careful about how they did their chores.

Coat Sails

The wind was so strong one winter day that the boys could make their coats into sails by pulling the bottoms up behind their backs. Sitting on their sleds on the snow-packed roads, they lifted their coats and started moving.

The oldest boy had the longest arms and the biggest coat so that when he raised the bottom of his coat up behind his head he had the biggest sail. The youngest boy with his short arms and small coat had the smallest sail, but he was so light that his sled slid more easily over the snow. When someone yelled Go! and the boys raised their sails, they knew this was a race that would not end until the wind had carried them half-way up a distant steep hill that had more slant than the wind had push.

The oldest and youngest boys took the lead. The other boys were worse off. They couldn't make their sails as big as the oldest boy's, and they were too heavy to slide as easily over the snow as the youngest boy.

It was no contest, really. The oldest and youngest boys went skimming along in a dead heat while the middle-sized boys coasted along like cars that were running out of gas. Sometimes they nudged each other's sleds down the middle of the road saying ordinary middle-sized things like Who cares? and They'll probably get hurt, and Just wait til the wind dies down, and At least we have company.

The Boys Learn to Use Wire

Sometimes a sow couldn't have her young. They'd catch in the tight opening of her womb.

When the men saw this happening, they called the boys. The boys' small hands and thin arms were just right for reaching deep into the sow to where the pigs were stuck.

First one boy soaped-up, rubbing soap on one hand and arm up to his shoulder. Then he'd go in shoulder-deep to find the little snout. When he felt the snout, he'd pinch it between his fingers.

The problem was that both his hand and the pig snout were slippery and he couldn't hang on if the pig was stuck very tight at all.

Then one of the boys got the idea to use a heavy wire as long as his arm with a little hook at the end that slipped over his forefinger. He went in with this and hooked the pig under the chin.

The other boys helped, pulling the wire from the outside.

Sometimes the wishbone jaw shattered and the pig died, but when it worked the pig came fast. The boys hurried to pick it up and put it bleeding to the sow's teats.

That little bit of pain made the pig lively from the start and the blood quickly got washed away by that fresh white milk.

Big Boots

In the winter, the youngest boy wore five-buckle boots that were much too large for him. The looseness of the rubber boots left gaps at the top where they should have fit tight against his calves. They fit so loose that his legs rubbed against the cold rubber as he walked, rubbed and let in cold air and snow. Soon his legs, from his ankles to his knees, became chapped, and when he took his socks off at night his legs looked and felt as if they had been sunburned.

The youngest boy did not complain, though he noticed that none of the other boys had chapped legs when they went to bed.

He learned that Vaseline rubbed on at night would let the skin recover just enough so that his legs looked normal in the morning when he pulled his socks on and then the high and loose rubber boots. Every day that he wore the boots, he could feel he was slipping behind, and that every night his legs were just a little more chapped than they were the night before. After a while, there were cracks on his skin so deep that they left patterns like those on the shell of a turtle.

On some mornings he could feel the pain starting already when he slipped his socks on, but he still chose the big boots, even though a smaller pair sat beside them in the porch in case he wanted to step down into a size that fit him. It was tempting, but as soon as he shuffled along through the snow leaving those enormous tracks behind him, he'd notice the looks on the others' faces that he was sure were looks of amazement and adoration, so he knew he could endure until spring.

3 ❖❖❖❖❖❖❖

Chicken Pox

One spring the boys all got chicken pox and had to stay home from school so they wouldn't give it to anyone else.

After a few days, when the scabs were starting to form, they felt just fine, except for the itching. But the grown-ups still wouldn't let them go to school, so they figured it was a good time to learn how to do something new. One of them looked at a bird book and learned how to draw bird pictures. Another took up embroidery. One decided to make baskets out of grass. Another started playing music on a recorder.

Some girls from school who had already gotten over their chicken pox came by to see the boys while they were working. They teased the boys that they were doing things that girls do.

The boys didn't feel like fighting back, so they just showed what they had done. The boy who was embroidering held up a dishtowel he was working on. All the stitches were on the line and very tight. Even the French knots. Then another boy held up his pictures of ducks. They were so good that the girls thought he had traced them. The grass basket another boy had made was woven so tightly that when he held it up to the light the girls could not even see a peephole. And the boy with the recorder played "Yankee Doodle" without missing a note.

The mothers sat in the next room talking about a vaccine for chicken pox. Wouldn't it be a shame, said one of the mothers, if someday boys never get sick enough to learn how to do those things?

The Robin's Nest

Their grandfather was going to show them where a robin had built a new nest in the grove. They walked along, staring up into the leafy branches, when one of the boys tripped on something. His Ouch! made everyone's eyes look down instead of up.

Until now it had been such a quiet and easy day, with the sun and breeze mixing together like whipped cream and sugar and spreading a sweetness over everything and everybody. Seeing the robin's nest with its pale blue eggs would have been what this day was all about. And now this.

The boy who tripped sat down and grabbed his foot.

Something sharp stuck out of the ground, a rusty pointed thing.

This is where we used to bury old equipment we didn't need any more, said their grandfather. That's the tooth of an old dump rake trying to sneak back into the world.

The boy who had tripped saw that the others were finding the metal tooth more interesting than his misery. He got up and helped them pull on the tooth, which was curved like a sliver of moon—and when they pulled, it was as if they were unzipping the earth, which split open, and plant roots frayed out from the wound like tiny threads.

Look at that, said their grandfather. He kicked at the dirt they had loosened. He knelt down and started into the dirt. Look, he said, and held up what looked like a bent horseshoe. This is called a twisted clevis, he said.

He went back to digging. This is part of the knotter for the binder back in the days of threshing machines. And here's a piece of a corn shucker glove. See that little hook that would pull the husk back? And here's the sediment bulb off an old tractor.

The grandfather was acting like a dog going after a hidden bone, scratching away with his strong old hands as if digging up and naming this useless junk was good for something.

This here is from an old harrow, he said. Those there from a cream separator. Here's part of a stanchion lock. That's from a double-tree. See this? It's a gear from a derrick for lifting the fronts of wagons off the ground.

The boys watched and listened. What their grandfather was doing didn't make much sense. If you're going to throw things away and bury them, why not forget about them and do what you were going to do—which was find that robin's nest? But they waited, and after a while they could see that their grandfather must have gotten what he needed. He shoved dirt back over what he had dug up, brushed off his dirty hands, and looked up into the tree branches with them.

It sure is a nice day, he said. Perfect for finding a robin's nest. Now be quiet. We don't want to scare her away.

Who Had Good Ears

This boy had such good ears that he heard sounds others did not hear. Many of the sounds were bad sounds, like the squealing of a piglet that had been stepped on by its mother or the moaning of electrical motors drying the corn. Even the buzzing hum of fluorescent yard lights caught his ear, keeping him awake, grating on his nerves. Bad sounds made him jittery and made him a bad listener when grown-ups told him to settle down. After hearing so many other bad sounds, the grown-up voices came across to him like so much static on a poor radio channel.

But the boy with good ears also heard sweet sounds, like the breeze in the box elder tree outside his bedroom or the tiny waterfall sounds of the drainage tile emptying into the creek. While others heard the train whistle, he heard the musical clicking of the wheels on rail joints. He heard the path of silence left behind the train. He heard the weeds lean from the whoosh of air. He heard the ripple in a stream. He heard little symphonies in the ice-bound twigs rattling in the wind. But mostly what the boy heard were the songs of birds. While others heard airplanes overhead, he heard the meadowlark far in the distance. When others heard traffic on the gravel road, he heard pigeons in the barn eaves. The good sounds of birds were a warm bath to him, calming him down and making him a good listener when grown-ups told him what to do.

Because bird songs were his favorite sounds, he spent hours listening to them. Alone and silent behind bushes or fences, he was their best audience. But the day came when listening was not enough, and he started answering the birds as best he could. He started at night when only the owl was singing. Hooting like an owl was as easy as playing a penny whistle, and the owl responded by answering back. During the day, he went on to the more difficult songs of other birds, and what he found with the owl was true with the other birds too: when he answered them, they answered back. To him, their answers sounded like applause.

Not all bird songs were easy, he soon learned, but he practiced long and hard. Everyone told him he was good at bird songs. The birds seemed to agree. They were a kind audience, sometimes fluttering by to get a closer look at him when he was finished with his little concerts.

Encouraged by his success, he expanded his repertoire. Crow sounds he mastered in a day, though his good ears had some trouble telling him that either the crow's or his own cawing fell in the good sound category. In less than a week he had the blue jay down. The staccato chirps of the sparrow came easy for him, as did the predictable repetitions of the chickadee. But then came the cheek and lip-tightening demands of the gold finch and the air-swallowing gurgle of the pigeon. He went from bird to bird, changing the instruments of his fingers and lips and tongue to meet the challenge of each new audience. Sometimes a bird with high standards showed some signs of impatience with his imperfect renditions and, like a fussy choir director, repeated the song over and over in an effort to help him get it right.

Success at bird calling led to fantasies of larger audiences. Singing back to large flocks of ducks and geese seemed foolish, since he wanted to sound like a musician, not a hunter. He sought out huge flocks of starlings, but starlings either lacked patience or good taste and would flee at even his best imitations. He studied bird books and imagined traveling to exotic islands that were covered with colorful birds whose songs must be as varied and challenging as their colors. He was happy in his fantasies, but he had to live with the audience he could find on the farm.

He started roaming the fields, hoping to find every possible candidate: pheasants, quail, and what he could only think of as the little brown birds that fluttered in roadside ditches. Then, just when he felt he had exhausted both audience and repertoire, he had one terrible experience that changed everything. He had moved well beyond owl and crow, beyond sparrow and pigeon, beyond barn swallow and chickadee, and even beyond the complex riffs of meadow lark and brown thrasher. But he made the mistake of wandering into the dark marshes of the red-winged black birds. He practiced for an entire mosquito-ridden afternoon and thought he had almost made an audience of the one he was imitating, when, with no warning, he was attacked from behind by a red-winged blackbird who lit into his hair like an eagle into a nest of field mice.

It was his first lesson in performing to an audience that did not like what it heard. Perhaps bored. Perhaps irritable. Perhaps threatened that he was upstaging them. He didn't stop making bird songs, but he could never put his fingers to his lips again without remembering that moment, no matter what his own good ears were telling him.

The Parrot

You didn't see something like this every day—a green and red parrot flying across the hog yards and landing on the pointy-topped metal grain bin. Just perching there and squawking as if it owned the place, as if it thought it could carry on like a noisy angel on top of a Christmas tree or something.

All the boys saw it. All the boys heard it. Look at that thing! they yelled. Then they ran to the house where the grown-ups were having afternoon coffee. Everyone ran outside to see and hear what the boys saw and heard. The parrot was gone.

It was big and green and yellow and red! shouted one of the boys.

And it went like SQUAWK! SQUAWK! said another. It was right there on top of that metal grain bin.

But the parrot wasn't right there, or anywhere, and the grown-ups didn't have much patience with the idea of a parrot flying around the hog yards or perching on a grain bin. It wasn't even close to April Fool's Day, so this kind of nonsense, making everybody run outside for nothing, wasn't something they wanted any more of, did the boys understand that?

The grown-ups went back to the house to finish their coffee, but the boys set off to find the parrot which, so far, had done nothing but get them in trouble. They figured anything that big with so many colors on it, and with such a loud squawk, should be easy enough to find. When they first saw it flying over the hog yard, it hadn't really flown all that fast, and it flapped its wings so hard that it probably couldn't have gone very far without needing to stop to catch its breath. They started by looking in the grove. Then they checked every barn and shed. Sometimes they stood and listened, waiting for the parrot to give itself away. Nothing. No red, green, or red feathers. And not a sound except the ordinary sounds of the sparrows chirping and the pigeons oo-googling and the pigs scruffing around and the electrical transformer humming a little.

At supper nobody talked about the parrot. The next day the boys went looking for it again. Not a flutter. Not a squawk. They talked about the parrot among themselves, how big it was, how bright the colors were. They wondered if the hogs had seen it, and what they might have thought of it. They wondered if the parrot had flown over the cows, and what the cows would make of seeing a parrot in the pasture. And what would a pigeon or sparrow think when it saw the parrot? Would something as strange as a parrot on the farm be able to make friends with any of the animals?

A few days later, when they still hadn't seen any sign of the parrot, they started wondering what else it might have been. Could it have been a crow or something with some sort of colorful cloth it had picked up somewhere? Maybe a little girl's bright sweater? But what about the squawking? No birds around there made that kind of noise. When they weren't talking to each other about the parrot or whatever it was, they started wondering if they had seen or heard anything at all.

Have You Ever Seen
a Sad Sparrow?

The boys were bored. They walked around the farmyard. Most of the animals were sleeping or eating. Over the fences beyond the farmyard the corn and oats grew quietly. The only living things that seemed busy were the sparrows. And they were everywhere. Ruffling in the dust near the granaries. Bathing in the stock tanks. Singing from the weather vanes and cupolas.

Have you ever seen a sad sparrow? asked one of the boys. Look at them. They act like they own everything.

Sparrows were busy building nests under barn eaves. Sparrows were scavenging spilled feed from the pig troughs.

And they don't bother anybody either, said another boy. How do they do it?

The boys walked around the farmyard again, this time watching the sparrows more closely than ever.

Sparrows were riding on the backs of old cows, teasing bigger birds by flying just over their wings, mating on the hay stacks in little bursts of feathers and dust.

The boys wandered into the grove and, still looking up at the sparrows, stumbled over some old tires. Look, said one of them. Nobody is using these old tires. Let's do something with them.

What about that old cable in the tool shed? Nobody is using that. Let's tie these tires together.

They linked a half dozen old tires together with the cable. One boy climbed to the top of a cottonwood tree with a pulley, and together they hoisted the string of old tires up. They tied one end of the cable to a high branch. Now the linked tires hung down from the tree like a big necklace.

The boys used their new toy as a many-tiered swing. As a ladder. As a tree house. Or just as a comfortable place to sit and watch the rest of the world. Sometimes they got into different tires and made them weave and look like a dragon standing on its tail.

When the grown-ups got up from their naps, the boys told them about the swing they had just built. The grown-ups agreed it was a good toy and wasn't using anything that anybody needed. By the time the boys got back to their new swing, sparrows were already building nests in the hollows of the top two tires. The boys agreed that the sparrows should have the top two tires for themselves, since they had given the boys the idea for the tire swing in the first place. Fair is fair, they figured.

Uncle Jack and the Ducks

One summer day Uncle Jack visited the farm. The boys remembered how stupid he acted from last year's visit when he didn't know how to fasten his shoelaces and had his hat on backwards.

Maybe he has grown some brains since last year, one of the boys suggested. After Uncle Jack had some coffee with the grown-ups, the boys decided to test him.

Uncle Jack, would you like to see the pigs?

Oh, yes, he said. I would like that very much, and he wiped one of his big ears with his handkerchief.

Instead of leading Uncle Jack to the pig pens, the boys led him to the pond where the ducks were. The ducks started quacking as the boys came nearer with Uncle Jack.

They certainly sound like interesting pigs, said Uncle Jack.

Oh, you wait and see, said one boy and led Uncle Jack closer.

My goodness, they're walking on two little yellow legs with webbed feet—now those are some interesting pigs! said Uncle Jack.

One duck opened its bill for some food.

Oh, look at that mouth, said Uncle Jack, just the right size for a nice healthy pig.

All our pigs are like that, explained the boys.

Why, I declare, said Uncle Jack, who then sat on a fence post and sang the boys this song:

> *The pig is swimming like a duck*
> *and if it has a preacher's luck*
> *'twill soon grow wings upon its back*
> *and learn to quack,*
> *yes, quack quack quack.*
> *A pig that waddles like a duck?*
> *Do old drakes wallow in the muck?*
> *If my name is Uncle Jack*
> *a pig can quack*
> *yes, quack quack quack.*
> *If ducks are pigs, then up is down,*
> *the swill is blue and the sky is brown,*

a needle is bigger than your aunt's haystack,
if pigs can quack
yes, quack quack quack.
If you get there before I do
with your feet in a hat and your head in a shoe,
at a place where the snow is midnight black
and pigs go quack
yes, quack quack quack,
Be sure you forget to sing this song
with a long one short and a short one long—
smile a smile behind your back
and the pigs will quack
yes, quack quack quack.

Sing another song! Sing another song! shouted the boys.

Not right now, said Uncle Jack.

And with that he barked twice at the pigs before fluttering off down the road, and what looked like bits of down floated up from his shaggy coat.

See you next year, Uncle Jack! shouted the boys who had their own brains to look after.

What the Boys Did
about the Lightning

One stormy night a neighbor went outside to look at the sky. He stood under a clothesline. That was his mistake. He was struck by lightning and died.

The boys went to his funeral and, looking up at his face in the coffin, they saw that the insides of his nostrils were black. Not even the undertaker's powder and creams could hide what the lightning had done.

That was how the boys learned to hate thunder. It was thunder that sounded so interesting that the man walked out into the night where the lightning could find him. But the boys also heard the grown-ups talking about rubber. If only he had been wearing thick rubber boots, someone said. Rubber could have saved him.

That was all the boys needed to hear. They rolled rubber tires out of the grove where they were rotting under the huckleberries. They put a tire where people might go when they heard the thunder. They put one against the clothesline pole to protect anyone who might walk out like the dead man had done when he heard the thunder call. They leaned two of them against their house. That whole pile of old tires found new places to rot. Where they could do some good. The boys told everyone why they put the tires everywhere. So no one moved them.

To make sure that they were safe themselves, the boys brought one tire up into their room and set it in the window like a big wreath. Through the circle of that tire they watched and listened to many storms roar through the sky and pass them by without a spark of harm.

The Boys Learn about Water

People in America don't know anything about water, said the boys' grandfather who had moved from Holland when he was a young man. The boys liked it when he visited because he always had a story to tell, usually about something that was wrong with America.

They knew his rules. They were supposed to listen until he finished telling his story. Then he would ask them a question so they would have a chance to show what they had learned.

Let me tell you about water, he said, and the boys sat back to listen.

If you dig a hole and there's water nearby, you should stand between the hole and the water. Because if water sees the hole it's going to want to go there too. Water has eyes, you know. Very good eyes. That's how it finds its way around so well under the ground.

Now your ocean water, it has eyes too. In Holland,

men built dikes to hide the beautiful land. You know that story Americans tell about the Dutch boy who put his finger in the dike. Well, that little trickle of water wasn't going to hurt anybody. But that Dutch boy knew he had to keep his finger in the eye of the dike. You mustn't tempt water, you see. If the ocean water got a glimpse of that green grass of Holland, it would all want to be there too. In America you don't know these things. You think everything is blind except for the people who are trying to make it do what they want.

Now, boys, you've been on this farm your whole life—you answer this question. If you want water to stay in the creek, what should you do?

I know. Make sure the bank is so high that the water can't see over it, said the oldest boy proudly.

No! shouted the youngest boy.

What is your answer, little one? said the old man.

Pee in it, said the boy. Nothing can see if you pee in its eyes.

And if you had been that little Dutch boy in Holland, what would you have stuck in the dike? asked the old Dutchman with a twinkle in his eye.

Spitting Sally

One day the boys visited their cousin in town. They went with him to the town park where many town boys were playing. Some were shooting baskets on the cement court, some were sliding backwards down the high slide, and many were playing softball on the park diamond. But the boys were most interested in what was happening close to the horseshoe stakes. A girl about ten years old stood with her back towards the group of town boys who were throwing stones at her.

What's going on here? asked one of the boys.

That's Spitting Sally, said their cousin. She's not too bright. She's been in the third grade for three years. She always comes out here by the horseshoe stakes so kids can throw stones at her.

The boys walked closer to the girl. She had on a furry hooded coat and did not seem to be getting hurt when stones hit her.

Let's help her, said the oldest boy, who then picked up a stone and threw it at the town boys.

I wouldn't do that if I were you, said their cousin.

But another one of the boys already had picked up a stone too and threw it at the town boys. Let her alone! he yelled as he threw.

But while the boys were watching to see if their stones found their mark, Spitting Sally spat. A slimy mouthful of pink spit that smelled like pink peppermints almost hit both boys in their faces.

I warned you, said their cousin. If you don't know the game, you shouldn't try to play.

The town boys threw another volley of stones. Spitting Sally turned her furry back and through her wet pink lips giggled like someone at her own birthday party.

The Rooster and Hen Secret

Often the boys went into the yard to watch a rooster and hen mate. They had watched horses mate, and what happened there was no secret to them. The boar mounting the sow left little to be imagined. Dogs, cats, rabbits, sheep, and cattle had very open mating manners. There were no secrets with these animals. The boys could see what was happening.

But try as they did, crawling up behind roosters and hens, peering through knotholes and from behind wagons—from only a few feet away!—they could not figure how they mated. There were those ruffling feathers, the rooster's beak clamped to the comb of the hen, and the cloud of dust they made doing it. But what they were doing remained a great cloud of mystery.

Later, when the boys become men and find wives, when they sit alone at night with their wives in dark farmhouses on the plains, will they have to confess their ignorance of chickens? And will the wives forgive them their ignorance and confess that they too do not know? Perhaps then, as now, in the privacy of each other's eyes, they may suggest that perhaps no one knows how chickens mate.

Do you?

The Man Who Sharpened Saws

His old green truck had a soft bump to it when it came down the drive, but the man who sharpened saws was cruel. He'd kick cats or feed steel shavings to the chickens, if they bothered him. Usually they didn't— the boys cleared his way of chickens and hid the cats.

More than cruel, he was a communist. The boys heard that was how he really made his money, so they made him a song:

> *Bumpity bumpity*
> *Here comes the commie*
> *In his old green Chevy.*

Nobody asked him to come, but when he did, everybody brought their saws and watched him file in his easy way. That sound was music to the boys. At least, the nearest they ever heard to a violin.

When he finished his filing, he charged a dollar. Once he forgot even that.

That's how everybody knew he was a communist. And there were his tracts the boys might never accept, ones with big pictures of men with picks and shovels.

He's rotten to the core, said one of the men.

But the boys noticed how pure the saws glistened, and they'd celebrate his leaving by sawing wood. Any wood. It all was butter to them then.

By spring, when he was almost off their minds, the saws got dull, and the boys could hardly cut a willow branch to make a whistle. So they sang:

> *Bumpity bumpity*
> *NOW where's that commie*
> *in his old green Chevy!*

It was hard going with a dull saw, but one spring even the men talked about putting up signs to keep him away. And they would have, if they could have found saws sharp enough to make the signs.

The Great Strength

There were many strong men in that neighborhood. Ones who showed up at county fairs and wrestled a steer. Or went into the ring with the circus wrestler and threw him out in ten seconds. There were men who came to the sales barn every Saturday and took bets on what they could lift. Usually a young steer in one of the pens. Men who took on any two men in tug-of-war. Everyone knew who the strong men were and who to bet on.

But then there was the man nobody noticed. Who never tried showing off in front of people. He was the one with the great strength.

How could you tell who had the great strength? You couldn't. Not until there was an accident. Then he'd be there like the one good spring that never goes dry in a dry year. Just when you needed him he'd be there and not even smiling. Just doing what had to be done: pulling a hand free from moving gears, lifting a wagon off somebody's leg, pulling a hog from a well. Whatever had to be done.

The boys saw the great strength once. Late August when everything was quiet. All the oats harvested. All the straw stacked. Farmers in town visiting.

An old church was being torn down and people were standing around watching. The Caterpillar was pushing big pieces out of its side. All of a sudden the wind caught a piece of loose roof and lifted it off the church. It went wobbling through the air like a sick bird, then landed on one end and tipped over on a bunch of people.

When all you could hear was everyone's screaming, the roof started rising slowly, as if the wind had caught it again. It wasn't the wind. It was the great strength, in old overalls, lifting that big section of roof. All of those trapped people were crawling out scratched and bleeding.

Afterwards, everybody was looking out for the people who got hurt under the roof, and after a little while no one knew for sure where the great strength had gone. He was like the wind in this way too.

Who Stole Things

One man walked around at night and when people were not at home, he went into their houses and took things. Little things. Cookies. A doily from a coffee table. A bathroom towel. An egg or two. Maybe a pair of old pliers. He might have done this for years without anyone noticing, except that he never used anything he took. So things started cluttering up his house and tool shed, and people saw them when they visited. What's more, his wife was a worrier and asked people if they needed their things back.

In other ways the man was like everyone else. He even taught Sunday School. He also was a good farmer and knew more than most about curing sick chickens.

The boys knew he stole things. They didn't think it was fair that he could steal without being punished, and they didn't like him for it. So one night they went over to his place, and when the lights went out in his house, they sneaked into his tool shed and took a handful of shingle nails. But when they were sneaking out, the man caught them. He must have known what kind of noises a thief makes, so he was waiting for them by the tool shed door.

First he made them put the shingle nails back—he knew just where the boys had found them. Then he gave them all a spanking. With a paddle he had stolen two years before!

Now be good boys and go home, he said.

The boys ran home crying and saying, It's not fair!

When they told their story at home, they got another spanking, even harder than the man had given them, and were sent to bed without another word about it.

Buttermilk Pop

FOR JOYCE HEYNEN

So it was something they ate in the old country, so what? Nobody over here even knew how to pronounce its real name anymore. Over here they called it buttermilk pop. You can be sure they didn't call it anything like that in the old country. In the old country people probably called it something you wouldn't dare to say in polite company.

The boys didn't like buttermilk pop, and it didn't help matters to watch how it was made. It wasn't even real buttermilk. It was regular milk with some vinegar in it. Then some flour was stirred in there, along with an old egg and a couple handfuls of raisins. The whole mess was cooked until it was thick as leftover oatmeal. By this time it was slimy too, and looked like it would make better wallpaper paste than food. Big globs of it were spooned into the boys' bowls where they could pour on some thick molasses to make it look even worse. This was supposed to be supper, and they were supposed to fold their hands and thank God for their daily bread. Daily bread? That would taste like ice cream after this stuff.

The boys never cleaned their bowls on buttermilk pop nights. But before their bowls were half empty they'd say, Give me a little more of that buttermilk pop. They didn't really want more, but if the cooking pot wasn't emptied, the leftover buttermilk pop might end up on the supper table again tomorrow night.

Give me a little more, they'd say, and then stir it up good to make it look even more disgusting, and they might leave a half-eaten spoonful on top to make sure nobody would get the idea of serving any of it again.

After supper on buttermilk pop nights, it was the youngest boy's job to carry the garbage bucket out to the pigs. The bucket was heavier on buttermilk pop nights. The youngest boy would empty the bucket down the middle of the pig troughs, then slap away any pigs that tried to get more than their fair share. The pigs loved buttermilk pop and fought each other to get at it.

The youngest boy stayed with them to make sure

they all got some. He'd watch them go for it—every gooey strand, every bloated raisin, every smear of left-over molasses. How those pigs loved buttermilk pop! And how the youngest boy loved to see them eat it. He'd watch closely as their snouts cleaned out the corners and crevices of the feed trough. He'd wait until it was all gone. He'd just stand there with his mouth watering, thinking about pork chops.

Uncle Jack and the Compass

The boys went into town one Saturday night and met Uncle Jack at the Laundromat. It was the one place in town where the gum machine sometimes gave little prizes, and when they met Uncle Jack there he always gave each of them a coin to try their luck. But, as usual, it was only Uncle Jack who got a prize with his gum, this time a small compass with the figure of a duck on it. The head of the duck was the needle, pointing north. The boys got only gum.

You always get everything, said one of the boys. You're everybody's pet. You're even the gum machine's pet.

But Uncle Jack was not listening. He laid his little compass on his palm and followed the "N" arrow across the Laundromat. It pointed him toward the only washing machine that was in use. It had a round porthole of a window, and clothing churned and bounced against the glass. An old fat woman stood next to the washing machine with her clothes basket. She was watching her clothes through the little porthole.

The old woman wore dirty tennis shoes and brown stockings rolled down around her ankles to look like dog collars. There were crusted scabs on her legs where she might have scratched flea bites. Her dress was a faded pink and looked as if it had been tan or white once and then washed with red. Her breasts were large and hung down, but she had her arms crossed in front of her and held them up. They bulged over her forearms and almost covered them. Her wrinkled face was spotted with moles and dark patches. She had her gray hair tied up on her head, but strands of it had come loose and hung like little broken branches over her ears.

Uncle Jack stood next to her with his compass and looked into the washing machine too. Inside were nothing but underpants, brassieres, and underskirts. And they were bright flashy colors with flower designs. Red roses and yellow pansies bounced against the window of the machine.

And who are you, my pet? asked the old woman.

I'm the lucky one, said Uncle Jack. I got a compass with my gum.

And what are you looking for, my lucky one? said the old woman, letting down her arms and breasts.

I'm looking for North, he said.

And has your lucky compass found it in my washing machine? she asked.

If flowers fly north in the spring, he said. It seems to be attracted that way.

The old woman chuckled and drooled a little. Yes, yes, she said. Flowers fly north in the spring. As she laughed, more and more pieces of flowered underwear appeared, dancing inside the washing machine, flashes of color like so many flower petals in a spring breeze.

Go to the Ant, Thou Sluggard

It occurred to the youngest boy, early in the morning when his mind was still swimming in daydreams, that there were two kinds of people in the world. It came to him very clearly: there are people who are always trying to give something, and there are people who are always trying to get something. Givers and getters, he called them in his daydreaming mind. His grandfather was a giver. If you saw him coming, you knew he had something to give, maybe some advice, maybe something he had made for you. A neighbor across the section was just the opposite. He was a getter. He was the one who mowed the grass along the railroad track because he could get that hay free. No wonder people called him a go-getter.

The youngest boy talked about his giver and getter ideas over breakfast.

The other boys laughed at him. There are two kinds of people in the world, said one, people who can find their socks and people who can't. The youngest boy knew which kind he was.

No, said another, there are two kinds of people in the world, people who are so stupid that they think there are only two kinds of people in the world, and people who aren't that stupid.

Maybe there was another set of two kinds of people, the youngest boy thought: the ones who make fun of and the ones who get made fun of.

The grown-ups put a stop to the talking. You want to talk about getting and giving? All of you *get* ready for church or we'll *give* you something to think about.

Good thing it was a Sunday, so the youngest boy could have plenty of time to be by himself, inside his own mind, while the preacher preached.

But the preacher said something so loud that the youngest boy couldn't daydream himself away from it: Go to the ant, thou sluggard, consider her ways and be wise.

That probably meant there were two kinds of people in the world: lazy people and workers, but would the workers be the givers or the getters? the youngest boy wondered.

There was an ant hill in the grove, so the youngest

boy went to the ant that afternoon to consider her ways. All the ants looked like real go-getters, just like the neighbor who tried to get his hands on everything he could get. But the ants didn't seem to be getting anything for themselves, they were hurrying back home to give what they got, maybe even to the sluggards somewhere deep inside the little world of their ant hill.

There are three kinds of people in the world, the youngest boy announced over supper: people who get, and people who give, and people who get to give.

Where did he pick *that* up? said one of the grownups.

Fewer Cats Now

Fifty cats were not too many on the farm. Sixty or seventy, it was all right. They were worth their weight in cream. Plenty of cats meant more corn in the corn crib. Because cats ate the rats. Rats ate too many times their weight in corn. Cats were worth whatever they ate. Besides the rats.

This was before rat poison. Rat poison cost less than cream for the cats. And worked faster. Cats were like people that way, and rat poison was like machines. So rat poison was in and cats were out. The only thing was—boys couldn't play with rat poison.

So they couldn't make parachutes for the cats anymore and drop them from the top of the windmill. They used to do that—a harness and twine and feed sacks. This worked pretty well for most of the cats. For the ones that liked it. For the ones that purred when they were carried up the ladder to the top. These were the ones that didn't fight back when the boys dropped them from the top. They had a good ride down and were happy to do it again.

Some of the cats fought when they were falling and tried to climb up the parachute. That killed them. But there were so many cats in those days that nobody missed one if it got killed this way. That was before rat poison.

Now the cats get spayed because there is no reason to have so many. There are so few that if one got killed in a parachute, everyone would ask, Where is that cat? Lots of rat poison and lots of corn, and the price of cream going up. Only two or three cats left, and they sit on the front porch. Eating cat food and getting sick a lot.

Sunday School

The boys went to a very strict church. In Sunday School after the morning service, they had to sit in assigned seats. During the hymn sing the Superintendent checked the seating chart, and anyone who was not present had to memorize Psalm 23, Isaiah 53, or I Corinthians 13.

Not many children liked the Sunday School Superintendent. When he asked the children to suggest a song during the hymn sing, one of the boys always yelled out Page 325. On page 325 was a hymn called "Lord, Dismiss Us With Thy Blessing." This made the Superintendent angry, but he never caught the boy who yelled Page 325.

Later the church got more modern, but the rules stayed strict. Now all the seats for Sunday School had big numbers painted on them and a camera on the ceiling took pictures automatically. Empty seats showed up as numbers in the picture, and anyone whose number showed had to memorize Psalm 23, Isaiah 53, or I Corinthians 13.

The boys decided to fool the camera. They took balloons to Sunday School, blew them up, and tied them to their seats. This way the numbers didn't show up in the picture. Pretty soon more and more children started tying balloons to their seats instead of going to Sunday School.

After many weeks an Elder of the church decided to visit Sunday School to tell the children how wonderful they were for their good attendance.

When he walked in the back, he saw a sanctuary full of balloons swaying back and forth over the seats, and behind the podium where the Superintendent was supposed to be was the biggest balloon of all swaying slowly on a thick piece of twine.

4 ✛✛✛✛✛✛✛

The Bad Day

One day everything went wrong.

Look at that pigeon! shouted one of the boys.

It was staggering near a pig feeding trough, touching one wing tip to the ground to keep from falling on its side.

Maybe it's the heat, said the oldest boy. They ran to the sick pigeon and caught it. It gagged as if it were going to choke. Its eyes glazed, and one eyelid didn't open again after it blinked.

Quick, the tank! the oldest boy shouted. They ran to the water tank with the dying pigeon, held its head back, and splashed handfuls of water into its open beak.

The water made the pigeon gag even more, but out came a large kernel of corn. Coughing up the kernel was like turning a switch on inside the pigeon, which panted and started beating its wings. In a few seconds it flew off, full of life.

That was stupid, said a grown-up who had been watching from the hog house. Don't you know pigeons are the only bird that drinks with its head down? You could have drowned it with its head tilted back like that.

The boys were going to explain, but they saw that the man was having a bad day. A sow had accidentally lain on another of its piglets, leaving only four from the litter of ten. The man picked up the limp body of the last casualty and flung it through the air onto the manure pile.

Another dead one, he said.

But when the piglet hit the manure pile, out came a grunting sound.

Hey! shouted one of the boys, but the man had already heard it and had run over to the piglet. He held its snout in his hand and blew into its nostrils, then lay it on his knee and patted its small rib cage. The steady tapping was so much like applause that the boys clapped their hands. In a few seconds the piglet squealed and struggled to get away.

I wonder if that will teach you to get out of the way next time, scolded the man as he put the piglet back in the pen with its mother.

What a bad day, the man said. He kicked a pig trough to show what a bad mood he was in. A mouse that had been stuck under the trough scurried away with its tail bleeding.

Well, at least the cats have it good, said one of the boys, trying to cheer the man up. They looked at the four cats that were sleeping on their fat bellies in the alleyway. But then they woke up too and sniffed the air, as if bad luck had an odor to it.

The Goose Lady

Down the road lived an old lady who kept geese in her house. She lived upstairs and the geese lived downstairs. It was funny driving by in a car and honking because this made the old woman and geese look out their windows at the same time. All those long goose necks popped up in the downstairs window and the old lady's head popped up in the upstairs window. The old lady's neck was long too, and she wore a hat—even in the house—that made her head look like a big goose head.

During the day the lady went out into her orchard and picked weeds. She also picked up leaves and little sticks that fell from the trees. Lots of times the geese followed her around in the orchard, looking in all the spots where she picked things up to see if maybe she was really finding food.

The boys were supposed to stay away from the goose lady's house because she was crazy. The boys weren't so sure about that, so they went over there anyhow and watched the goose lady from the ditch.

Something you couldn't hear driving by in a car was that the goose lady was singing.

> *Lowly geese, by my side,*
> *How my sorrow I do hide,*
> *In the shivering of the leaves,*
> *In the whining of the bees.*
> *Lonely geese, tell me why*
> *You never reach toward the sky,*
> *Where the wind can set you free*
> *From earth, and free from me.*
> *Lovely geese, do you know*
> *That the one I once loved so*
> *Much more than my old eyes tell*
> *Turned his face and bade farewell?*
> *Lowly geese, by my side,*
> *How my sorrow I do hide,*
> *He left me nothing but an egg*
> *And prayed I'd never beg.*
> *Lovely geese, you've served me well*
> *With eggs to eat and down to sell,*
> *Ever close at my side,*
> *How my sorrow you do hide.*

Yep, she's crazy, whispered one of the boys. So they slipped away without the goose lady seeing them.

And when they went back, all they did was listen, and later would practice singing the goose lady's song whenever they were doing things they didn't like to do.

The Man Who Kept Cigars in His Cap

One man kept cigars in his cap. When the boys sneaked up behind him during threshing and tipped it off, the cigars fell on the ground. This was very funny to everyone, until one day the man put a rat in his cap. It was a rat the man had fed eggs so it was friendly to him.

When the boys tipped off his cap this time, the rat jumped to the ground and frightened them so much that they screamed and looked foolish.

The oldest boy said, He can't do this to us! We're boys from Welcome Number Three! Which was their township and schoolhouse number.

So they found a big tom cat that liked to kill rats. They took a striped engineer's cap like the cigar man wore and put a rubber rat under it and taught the tom cat to find the rat.

After a while they went walking toward the threshing machine where the man was working. One of the boys carried the tom cat on his shoulder, and no one paid attention when they walked behind the man. The tom cat saw the engineer's cap and jumped at it as the boys had taught him to do.

But instead of a rat, the man had put a skunk under the cap. It was an orphan skunk the man had fed milk when it was a baby, so the skunk was friendly to the man.

When the tom cat landed on the man's hat, the skunk let go its spray in the cat's eyes and on the heads of the boys. Everybody laughed at the boys as they ran away to the stock tank screaming and crying.

When the boys had cleaned themselves, the oldest one said, He has made us look like fools again. Let's do something to keep him from making everyone laugh at us.

So they started practicing with their sling shots and practiced until they could hit a tin can from thirty yards. They crawled behind a fence where no one could see them.

The man had put an owl under his hat, thinking that this time the boys would have a weasel. It was an owl he had helped in winter when its eyes were frozen shut so the owl was friendly to him.

When the man was not expecting it, the boys shot their stones at his cap. The stones hit the cap, some going through the cloth and through the feathers of the owl, killing it.

No one scolded the boys for killing the owl. Everyone agreed that the man had been asking for trouble right from the start when he put cigars in his cap.

Who Made Her Husband
Do All the Work

There was a woman down the road who made her husband do all the work. Not just the chores and field-work but the housework too. When he finished milking the cows, she might help him carry the milk in, but only so that he would get to the house a little sooner to cook supper. On Monday mornings she got up early to make coffee, but only so that he would awaken in time to do the wash before going out to feed the pigs. If she was busy, you could be sure it was only to make him busier. Most of the time she sat in her rocking chair next to the kitchen window looking out to see that he was doing the work she had told him to do.

In time, the husband came to be very lean and haggard while the wife was plump and cheerful. Some people said she was just plain working him to death. But these were not the people who knew the rest of the story. The part that started every night when this woman sent her husband out to a small shed next to the house to wash eggs. He would shuffle out there after his long day's work, turn on the one bare light bulb, and sit down under it on his small stool. In a half-circle around the stool he had several buckets of eggs that he had gathered during the day. Now he hummed to himself as he carefully washed each egg with a wet dishcloth and placed it in the large egg crate.

When the boys saw the light go on, they ran over to his little shed to hear this lean and tired man tell stories as nobody could tell stories. Within an hour after the light was turned on, the shed was packed with grown-ups and kids who came to listen to his stories.

The one about the chicken with three legs! one of the boys would shout, or How about the one about the lady who wouldn't cut her fingernails?

He'd tell them their favorite stories and then, every night, add one or two new ones. Sometimes the boys tried to help him wash eggs as he was talking, but he never let them. He knew just how long he wanted the stories and egg-washing to take. And the boys knew that the last story was about to end when he was washing the last egg.

While he was telling his stories, his wife sat in her rocking chair, watching people come from all over the neighborhood. She always had her note pad on her lap where she wrote down all the work she had planned for her husband the next day. Now and then she smiled as she looked out toward the shed, as if what was happening there was part of her plan too.

Strange Smells in the Night

One night the boys were getting ready for bed.

I smell a girl, said the youngest boy.

There aren't any girls here, silly, said the oldest boy.

They started looking anyway. Under the beds and inside drawers. One of the window curtains moved a little and the youngest boy said, See, there! That was a girl!

But there were no arms or feet, only the curtain moving a little. The boys went to bed without finding the girl. Still, they could not sleep because they could smell the girl. The smell got stronger.

After a while, in the dark, one of them said, It's not a girl, it's a lady. It smells like a grown lady.

They turned on the lights and looked for the lady. But she was not there.

Back in bed, they lay listening and smelling the strange smell. It's not a girl or a lady, one of them said. It smells like an old, old woman.

Again, the boys turned on the lights. The curtain was still moving. This time they saw something. It was dust, blowing in through the window. So they closed the window and went back to bed.

After that, they fell asleep.

Ducks and Bacon Rind

Well, everyone always told the boys not to feed bacon rind to the ducks, but nobody told the boys why not.

So they took some raw bacon rind and threw it to the ducks. A big duck swallowed it. The boys followed that duck around, watching to see what would happen. The duck looked all right.

But then the duck stopped, ruffled its wings, and passed the piece of raw bacon onto the ground as quickly as if it had laid an egg. Up waddled another duck and swallowed the bacon rind. Soon this duck passed it, and another duck quickly swallowed it.

This went on for a while, and the ducks learned to follow the last duck that had swallowed the rind, waiting for it to come out so they'd have their turn at it.

The boys watched the bacon rind being passed around from one duck to another in this way until one of them got an idea.

Let's tie a string to the bacon, he said.

The other boys looked surprised when they saw in their minds what would happen.

The boys chuckled and ran to get some strong string. After they tied this to the rind, they went back to the ducks. The first duck swallowed it, then the second, and so on, until the boys had all the ducks on the string. They held it tight, pulling the bacon rind tight against the bottom of the last duck.

Later the boys told this story to the men.

That would make a good story to tell some city slickers, said one of the men. They're the only ones who'd believe it.

Spotty

There was a neighbor dog that had gotten its left front leg cut off by a hay mower. After that, it lunged along on its three good legs, trying to keep up with the world the way it had in its four-legged days. It couldn't catch rabbits anymore and didn't even try for the gophers, but it could herd calves and keep cats out of the milk house. Its bark was as loud as ever, and that was usually enough to scare the animals that weren't smart enough to know how easily they could outrun the three-legged dog.

The boys liked to visit the farm with the three-legged dog. They'd make fun of the way it walked and tease it by holding out a hand and saying, Shake hands, Spotty. Shake hands.

Spotty was such an obedient dog and so eager to please everyone that he tried to shake hands. But he always remembered just in time that he didn't have another leg to stand on and would catch himself before falling on his nose.

Then one day Spotty surprised the boys when they held out a hand and said, Shake hands. Spotty stood on his hind feet and offered his free paw for a friendly shaking.

Now the boys had to think of a new game for teasing three-legged Spotty. They tried patty-cake on him, slapping their hands together and coaxing, Come on, Spotty, patty-cake patty-cake.

Spotty seemed to be ready for this game since he already had learned to stand on his hind feet. He followed the boys' motions and started swinging his one paw to meet the paw at the spot where the other paw would meet if Spotty had another paw. Then it was as if Spotty realized the boys were making fun of him. He lay down and hid his nose under his good leg.

Look, said the youngest boy. We made him feel stupid. Look at him.

The other boys looked at Spotty with the same pitying eyes as the youngest boy's. He was right. Spotty was embarrassed. And Spotty's embarrassment spread like a cold chill across the boys. The smirks left their faces and they all blushed with their own embarrassment. They knew they would never ask this friendly three-legged dog to do something he couldn't do again. Spotty must have known it too. He pulled his nose from under his leg, stood up on his hind feet and held out his paw. But no more patty-cake.

Uncle Jack's Riddle

Uncle Jack had a way of appearing when he was least expected. Since he was not known for ordinary sense, it did not surprise anyone that he was unpredictable. No one knew what day Uncle Jack might show up— but then, he probably didn't either.

Hello there! came a voice through the boys' bedroom window early one very rainy summer morning. The boys were jittery since thunder and lightning had been coming and going all evening. Hearing that voice between claps of thunder was enough to startle them to their wits' end.

Hello there! came the voice again. It's a good day for mud pies!

The boys ran to the window. It was Uncle Jack! There he stood in the drive, wearing a black raincoat with a big hood on it. He looked more like a bear standing upright than like a human being.

Do you know what can go out in the rain without a cap on and not get its head wet? he shouted up to them.

It was another one of Uncle Jack's silly riddles. The oldest boy said, Uncle Jack did you really come all the way over here through the thunderstorm just to ask that stupid riddle?

A duck, interrupted the youngest boy. That was an easy riddle, Uncle Jack.

Wrong, little one. Not everything can be a duck. You guessed too quickly this time, said Uncle Jack. Now you'll have to listen to all the clues. And, still standing in the rain, Uncle Jack sang the whole riddle to the boys.

> *I have no legs,*
> *I have no arms,*
> *I wear no bracelets*
> *for my charms.*
> *I have no eyes,*
> *I have no nose,*
> *and when I rise,*
> *I wear no clothes.*
> *No whiskers have I,*

though I do have hair,
when I appear,
young women stare.
I start out small,
but then I swell,
not like the wind
or a steeple bell.
When the rains come down,
my head stays dry,
without a rain cap—
now what am I?

The boys couldn't think of any answers to Uncle Jack's riddle. What is it, Uncle Jack? We give up.

Why, it's a thunderhead, said Uncle Jack. I've been watching them all night. There's nothing but stars above them and it only rains beneath them, so the thunderhead must always be dry.

Uncle Jack chuckled and said, Whoever tells that riddle, his mouth will always be warm. With that he ran laughing down the drive.

The boys looked out the window at the large thunderheads. Say, said one of the boys, they don't have hair. Uncle Jack's riddle said,

No whiskers have I
but I do have hair.

Just then the sky lit up again with long wavy strands of lightning that reached to the ground.

Then there was thunder, which sounded very much like Uncle Jack's crazy laughter.

The Blind Pony

The pony was blind in one eye when it was born. At first it was easy to catch if you remembered which side to come up on. But after a while the ear on the blind side got strong from listening so hard for someone sneaking up on it. That ear got so good it would hear someone coming on the blind side farther than the good eye could see on the other.

So the boys had to think of new ways to catch the blind pony. First they tried trapping it in the corner of the pasture, but the blind pony always ran with its good eye towards the fence and its good ear towards the boys. This way it never ran into the fence and could still whip its head when it heard the lasso coming through the air. The blind pony was a good kicker too, and the boys learned not to try grabbing at it from behind.

Next the boys tried hiding in trees where the pony walked, thinking that they could drop a rope over its head as it passed under them. But it was as if the pony could hear that part of the tree where the leaves weren't rustling and wouldn't walk under a tree where one of the boys was hiding.

Finally, the boys tried coaxing the blind pony with apples.

Why didn't we think of this before! said one of the boys when this worked. Pretty soon the blind pony came at the sound of the boys climbing the apple trees. Its nose got strong too, and it could tell which boy had an apple in his pocket.

But the boys never did saddle or bridle it. They knew how dangerous it would be to ride a blind pony.

The Old Turtle

One day a farmer found a dead cow in his pasture. Its throat had been torn and slashed by something. The sheriff looked at it. The paper said something about it. Pretty soon everybody had a story about it.

The boys listened to the men talking—and one thing they heard was that a long time ago when that farmer was a boy on that same farm, he found a big turtle near the creek that ran through the pasture where the cow was killed. He told his father about it—and the two of them went out there with shovels and beat that big turtle's head on a rock. They left it there and weren't going to return until after sunset when they could be sure it was dead. Then, when it was safe to pick up that big turtle, they were going to make turtle soup out of it.

But when they came there after sunset, the turtle was gone. They found its claw marks in the mud along the creek where it had pulled itself back to the water. They didn't see it again.

Did that turtle come back twenty-five years later to get even? Kill a cow in that same pasture where its head had been beaten flat?

Sure enough. Somebody found that old turtle. Or at least saw it. Its head was like a dish pan, flat like that, and its jaws were a lot broader than they should have been. Everybody put one and one together.

You could read about this later in Ripley's "Believe It Or Not." That's the whole story.

The boys didn't talk about it much. It didn't have much to do with them since there weren't that many turtles left in the creeks anymore. Even Old Dish Pan Head would probably be dead pretty soon. Before it got any more cows. Cut worm or gopher poison would get in its water—or some new weed spray that hadn't been tested on turtles.

The Big Push

One morning the boys walked into the cow barn to find an awful sight. One of the cows had calved the night before, but during the night her womb had come out and was lying in the gutter behind the cow.

The oldest boy didn't gag or jump back, and he was the first to notice that the strange mass led into the cow. He stayed and watched while the other boys ran for help.

Then the work began. The womb had to be cleaned off with soap and kept clean so that the insides of the cow would not get infected. The hardest part was shoving the womb back in. Pushing the womb back in was like trying to push a calf back in—nothing inside the cow wanted things to go in reverse like that.

When the boys understood what they were working with, the womb in the gutter didn't bother their stomachs. First, they cleaned the gutter around the womb with pitch forks and then with water. They got down on their knees and started washing the womb, pulling the clean part up on their laps as they worked. When this was finished, they cradled the womb in a white sheet and got ready to help with the big push.

All of this took several hours and word got around the neighborhood. Even the mailman stopped in to see this and was ready to help push. The boys had to stand back, but the men's hands were so big that they couldn't get enough of them around the cow's vagina to tuck the womb in as they pushed.

So the boys got their turn. And they thought of something the men wished they had. One of them went around to the front and fed the cow some oats while the others pushed. Having things coming in from both ends at the same time must have confused the cow's instincts. When she was swallowing the oats, the boys behind pushed. The cow coughed the oats up but the womb was in. After that the cow ate the oats again without coughing it up. The womb stayed in too.

The boys thought they'd get a lot of praise for what they had done with the big push, but the men seemed to be more interested in never talking about that womb again.

The Injured Fawn

The boys were walking along a headline fence one summer day. In the grass they found a fawn that had crawled out of the alfalfa where a mower had cut off one of its hind legs and almost cut off the other.

The fawn lay its ears back, hiding, until it knew the boys saw it, then looked up and bleated like a hungry lamb. One of the boys looked for the cut-off leg in the alfalfa but couldn't find it.

They carried the fawn home and fed it milk from a calf bucket that had a rubber nipple on the bottom. After it was fed, the fawn tried to run away, as if it thought a little bit of milk would make its hind legs come back. And somehow it did manage one leap forward, but then fell on its side and didn't try to get up.

Pretty soon, the boys had to tell the men about the fawn they had found. They told the men they wanted to make a new leg for the fawn and sew back the one that was almost cut off. The men said they would help.

The wounds were cleaned with water and black horse salve. The one leg was sewn back and a wooden splint put on it. The other, which was only a stump, got a leather patch put over the exposed bone and a wooden leg the shape of a deer's strapped on.

The boys fed and played with the fawn all summer where it lived in the barn. Towards fall it was so good on its new legs that it jumped and ran, first playing with the boys and then always going for a door or window. The boys had to move quickly to keep it from getting away on its new legs.

With all its jumping and running, the fawn's legs got infected. Gangrene set in and it died.

Did anybody cry? Nobody cried. The boys buried the fawn in the orchard and kept the wooden leg to show people later how it had gotten worn smooth from the fawn's happy days of playing with them and trying to leap through windows for freedom.

The Flamethrower

The boys weren't supposed to play with matches. So when they did, they made the best of it by using them for their favorite games.

They liked to throw the match-sticks down head-first on the sidewalk and make them pop like little firecrackers. Or they made the heads just wet enough so that they gave off a stream of smoke like rockets when the boys shot them from a BB gun. But their favorite game was lighting each other's farts.

This was a tricky sport because it meant pulling your pants down and having someone hold a lit match very close to your bottom. The boys thought the results were worth the risk. The passed gas did not explode but did ignite like a torch with a quick blue flame.

The boys tried to see who could make the biggest flame. They were happy that the slowest runner and the one who was poorest at baseball at least could win at this game. He was a natural and didn't even have to practice at it. They called him the flamethrower, but always in a respectful voice. They knew that what he did to a match would never make the Guinness Book of Records, but at least it gave him one thing that he could do better than the rest of them.

Ground Squirrels

The first thing the boys did to get ground squirrels in the pasture was to find all the holes. This way one boy could pour the cream cans of water down one hole while the others waited at the dry holes with sticks.

Not everybody could get ground squirrels this way. You had to know what you were doing. If you made too much noise near the opening of the hole where you were going to pour the water, the ground squirrel might dam it up a few feet down the tunnel. You had to be quiet and you had to be fast. And you had to have a lot of water. If the water wasn't coming fast enough and if there wasn't enough of it, the ground squirrel would try to drink it as it came—or the ground would just soak it up before it could bother the squirrel. But if it heard and felt a tidal wave coming, it ran for light without pausing to talk with its friends about what to do.

There was one big old ground squirrel the boys had

been trying to get all summer. One time it must have heard them coming and dammed up the hole a few feet from the surface. When the boys tried pouring water down another hole, it beat them by damming that one up too. It must have followed the boys' footsteps from hole to hole, damming each one up just before the boys could pour water down it. Another time the boys were quiet enough, but the squirrel dug a low passage that emptied into the creek letting all the water run away while it remained safely in the higher tunnels. Getting that ground squirrel had become the project of the summer.

This time we're going to use five cans of water instead of three, said the oldest boy. We're going to make sure there are no low holes where the water will run out, and we're going to be perfectly quiet. We're not going to let it trick us by sticking its head out of one hole and coming out of another.

The boys watched for two afternoons before they saw the ground squirrel out in the open. It had grown even bigger than the last time they had seen it. One of the grown-ups saw it too and said it was the biggest one he had ever seen.

That critter must eat fifty dollars worth of corn a

year, he said. I'll give each of you a dollar if you get that one.

Now the boys knew they had to get the ground squirrel for sure. There was more than pride at stake, there was money. They waited and waited, watching it move from one part of the pasture to another until finally just before supper it slipped down a hole. Not only did the boys walk quietly, but they took only a few steps at a time, and then stopped a few seconds—the way a cow does when it is grazing. The youngest boy bent down when they were pausing and pulled off a few handfuls of grass to make their presence sound even more like a grazing cow.

When everyone was in place, one of the boys poured all five cans of water down the hole as fast as he could. The boys at the other holes were ready with their sticks and could even hear air coming out, the water was filling up the tunnels that fast!

Everything was going according to plan! Everyone was frozen in his place over a hole and ready with his stick for when that big gopher would be flushed out. It would only be a matter of a few seconds now, they were sure of it. Then water started spurting out of the ground all around the boys—ten times as many holes as there were boys. There! There! There! they shouted to each other as water spurted out of the ground, first one place then another, and then another!

The boys ran in circles, trying to figure out where the squirrel would try to make its escape. When the spurting stopped, they stopped too and all started to blush at once. Sure, they were Dutch, but they knew there were not enough thumbs in the whole world to plug all the holes this old gopher had made in the dam of their intentions. They heard a swishing in the grass, not unlike the swishing of a fish that knows its way around in its own pond.

The Old Policeman

One Saturday night when the boys went into town, they found a basement window of the church open. They gathered a basket of ripe tomatoes out of people's gardens, climbed into the church, went through the sanctuary, and up into the church steeple. From here they could throw ripe tomatoes at passing cars.

They hid behind the brick bulwarks at the base of the steeple cone, which reached twenty feet above them to the cross on the pinnacle and over a hundred feet over the street below them.

The first few throws were just target practice. The tomatoes took much longer to reach the street than the boys expected and landed ten feet behind the cars. Then they found their mark, and tomatoes splattered over windshields and hoods and car tops and trunks. Within minutes the police car came speeding to the scene.

The policeman stopped, turned on the flasher, and shone his spotlight on the bushes across the street. Look, said one of the boys. It's the old policeman.

There was some comfort in this. The old policeman was kind. And he was so slow that he never seemed to catch anyone. But he was very good with the spotlight and had a reputation for doing with the spotlight what he couldn't do with his legs.

Seeing that it was the old policeman, the boys were not afraid. One of them threw a tomato. No, the other boys warned in a loud whisper.

The tomato splattered right in front of the police car. The old policeman made a quick U-turn and the spotlight started running around under the bushes near the church like a coon dog with a hot scent. Then the spotlight made a few quick leaps up the church steps. The boys crouched behind the bulwarks. The spotlight jumped a few times, as if it were sniffing the air, and then ran straight up the side of the church and up to the steeple. It hopped over the boys' heads without touching them and zipped all the way to the pinnacle above them.

The old policeman aimed the spotlight right at the cross, and kept it there while the boys breathed heavy.

Then suddenly the light was gone and the police car drove away.

When they were sure the coast was clear, the boys hurried out of the church and back downtown. The police car was parked on the corner where it usually was when the old policeman was on duty. As the boys walked past the old policeman, they tried to look innocent. He just stared at the boys. Stared hard and acted as if it were below his dignity to say anything to them. As if he were some kind of preacher or prophet or something. The boys went to the gas station and washed their hands. Let's try something different next week, said the oldest boy.

The Boys Learn by Watching

Sometimes the farmers talked about the different ways they could tell if a sow was going to farrow. Anybody could see when a sow's belly was getting thick and her teats were getting full, but the trick was to be able to tell if the sow was going to start having her babies within the next few hours. This way the sow could be penned up so that when her pigs were born there would be no danger of them wandering off and nursing the wrong sow or of them getting stepped on by big pigs that were running loose in the hog house.

I just watch her until she starts building her nest, said one farmer. Then I know she's almost due. Never fails.

That doesn't work, said another farmer. I've watched a sow putting mouthfuls of straw in a circle for two days and still not farrowing. The only way you can tell for sure if she's about to farrow is if she gets a little puffy in the back and starts opening.

The boys listened to the men talk like this. But they knew the men were just teasing each other. They knew the men knew the only way you could tell for sure was when the sow was lying in her nest and you would come up and rub her bulging udder. If she was ready to farrow, she turned her belly and teats up as much as she could so that the hand that was rubbing them had an easier time of it. And if the teat hardened in the hand, and if the sow started grunting in a regular sort of beat, and if a bead of milk formed on the nipple without the hand pinching it— then you knew for sure she was going to farrow in a few hours.

The boys often hid and watched the men rubbing a sow's teats, saw how gently the palm touched and then the fingers. When the men left, the boys tried it and knew they were doing it right when the sow's low grunting sounded the same as when the men were rubbing her.

After they stopped rubbing, they cupped their hand the way the men had over a sow's teat, then stared into their palm the way an outfielder stares into his glove after he has caught a long fly ball. They stared into their palm proudly, as if they had put something important there, like a secret that would always be there if they needed it.

The Old Boar and the Pigs

One time a sow that had nine little pigs ate a piece of glass and died. Her pigs quickly started to wither. The boys did what they could to save those pigs—feeding them cow's milk from a bottle and giving them little bits of sod—but nothing worked. The pigs got scours, their hair got scruffy, and their hind legs got so weak that their rear quarters weaved when they tried to walk.

Then one night an old boar broke into the pen with the little pigs. In the morning he was lying with the sick little animals and grunting like a sow.

Get out of here, you stupid boar! one of the boys shouted.

But the old boar just growled and snapped at them.

Go on, you can't give them any milk!

The old boar didn't understand them. But when he saw that the boys did not dare to come into the pen with him, he lay down and turned his large belly toward the pigs the way a sow does.

The pigs nestled up against that old boar and started to suck on his useless little teats.

What a funny sight, the boys thought, though they were sure the pigs couldn't be getting any milk. But soon the pigs looked stronger than they had the night before. They fought over nipples and squealed like healthy little pigs. The boys didn't know what to think of this, but since the pigs were so happy with the old boar they let them alone.

The next morning the boys ran to the hog house to see how the old boar was doing with the pigs. The pigs were lying against his belly and he was snoring loudly. When he heard the boys, he stood up growling and all the pigs rolled off his belly into the straw, dead.

The old boar sniffed the dead pigs for a moment and then ate one. Soon he went back into the pig yard and lay down in a big wallow, grunting like an old boar again, but not mean anymore now that he had nothing to protect.

Death Death Death

One hot summer day the boys were wandering around the yard.

What's that smell? asked one of them.

Hog manure is what it is, said another.

No, look, said the first boy. It's that dead chicken.

Sure enough, there was a dead chicken lying near the chicken coop. It had been dead maybe a week and the sun had eaten most of its insides out.

Then another boy said, No, look. Maybe the smell is coming from that dead pig over there.

The boys walked over to the dead pig that was lying near the hog house. There were flies all over its body and going in and out of its nose and ears. It was only two days dead so the smell was not very strong yet.

Then another one of the boys said, I'll bet the smell is from that dead starling the cats killed and wouldn't eat. They walked over to the auto shed and found the dead starling, but it was almost dried out to a skeleton.

Death, Death, Death, said one of the boys.

There were dead animals all over the farmyard— if they'd look for them. Besides the rodents that were dead under the ground and they'd never see. Dead flies here and there. Dead grasshoppers in the tall grass. Dead bees. Dead ladybugs. Probably dead birds that were dying in their nests.

And this was not unusual. Things die. It's just that the boys happened to be noticing it all at once. Which happens in the summer. What was good about winter was that the snow hid dead animals and other dead creatures.

Look. One of the boys pointed to the sky. They were not alone, noticing all this death. A chicken hawk was circling overhead. Circling over the whole farmyard.

This place stinks like dead everything, said one of the boys.

There's only one thing to do about all this death, said the youngest boy. Clothespins.

So they put clothespins on their noses and ran off to play.

Uncle Jack and the
Beautiful Schoolteacher

Uncle Jack stopped to greet the beautiful school-teacher who lived in a mobile home on the school yard. He had seen her downtown shopping and noticed how gracefully her hands moved across the fabric in the dry goods store and how delicate their movement as she lifted an apple to the light in the supermarket. He felt there was a message to him in the way she touched things, but he was not sure what it was.

As Uncle Jack approached her small metal trailer house, he saw her outside hanging her wash on a rope that had been strung to a nearby tree. Even now, her hands seemed to dance like those of a deaf person talking to a lover. When she saw him, she stopped her work and smiled. Yes, she recognized him too.

You have amazing hands, said Uncle Jack.

I have noticed yours too, she said, and her eyes

moved to where they hung at his sides. They stood in the cool sunlight of that October day, staring at each other's hands. Then she held up her right hand in such a way that the shadow of a rose appeared on the shining white side of the trailer house.

Ah, yes, what a wonderful movie screen, said Uncle Jack. The petals of the shadow-rose quivered as if responding to the same breeze that was bringing color to their cheeks where they stood side by side. Then across the white screen came the shadow of Uncle Jack's right hand in the form of a butterfly, which lit pulsing on the rose.

Like a second movie being projected on the same screen, her left hand became a sunfish swimming through shimmering water, but the fingers of Uncle Jack's left hand became a net that caught the fish. While the sunfish of her left hand submitted to the net, the rose of her right hand extended into long fronds of a palm tree. This made the butterfly of his right hand knuckle into a camel that paused to rub its humped back on the trunk of her palm tree. Now the sunfish of her left hand emerged freely as a sailboat driven by a wind that their reddening faces showed had grown stronger, and Uncle Jack's left hand quickly extended into a palm of waves that carried the blithe boat on its undulant swells. Her right hand joined the waves of his left hand, and the sailboat of her left hand took wings to become a swan ascending toward the window of the trailer house where, in mid-flight, it met his right hand in the same swan shape, and they let their hands glide together into a large shadow from a cloud that was passing overhead.

With their shadows gone, they returned to themselves, to each other and the flesh and bone that was left of them.

You do have amazing hands, he said to her again.

As do you, she said.

And so, without saying any more, they parted to go their separate ways because she was, after all, a schoolteacher. And he was, after all, Uncle Jack.

The Boys' House

The smells of feedlots and weed killers were getting to the boys. Then there were the constant sounds of diesel tractors and electric feed augers. When the sun went down, things didn't get any better: fluorescent lights spraying light everywhere and the corn-drying blowers moaning through the night.

We need to make our own place, said the oldest boy. Let's build a house to get away from all this noise and stink and light.

They already had built secret hide-aways made out of hay bales in the barn loft, but they needed something that didn't end up being fed to the cattle.

And let's build close to water! shouted the youngest boy. Along the pond! Let's build our own house along the pond!

The dream of a place of their own perched on the edge of the pond started taking shape. It would be a sound-proof, a light-proof, and a smell-proof house that wouldn't get torn down when the cattle got hungry.

The grove was full of junk that the grown-ups had thrown away as the farm got modern. They found two-by-fours and shingles, plywood, tar paper and sheet metal, disk blades and harrow teeth, fly wheels and mower arms, bricks and cement blocks, old bottles and broken wagon wheels, pieces of a log chain, tin cans and rusted buckets, a car hood, axles, a cupola, pieces of a cream separator, washers, bolts, old tires, fence wire, gears and pulleys. A whole world of building material!

What took shape on the edge of the pond was like nothing ever before constructed by human hands or seen by human eyes. Thick as an army tank with cement blocks and bricks at the bottom, it bristled with sharp-edged metal blades and axles as it rose up. The boys made a jagged roof from the two-by-fours, the tar paper and the sheet metal, and set the cupola on top of it all.

Let's use all the stuff so we don't have to carry anything back to the grove, said the oldest boy.

They did. Shingles filled in spaces between blades and spikes and axles. A piece of chain hung next to the front opening as a door bell. They tied the tires together and lay them at the edge of the pond to look like a dock in front of a lake cabin. Inside big chunks of metal from different pieces of equipment became chairs. They had a plywood bed. They had a car-hood table for eating and playing cards.

When they had used up all the material, they decided they must be finished. They walked back a ways and looked at what they had done. It might have been a war machine made by some pretty tough people a long time ago. Or a scarecrow invented by some survivalists to keep away nosy space travelers. One thing for sure: it looked like the kind of place no outsiders would want to mess with. The cattle must have looked at the boys' house too, because they had all walked to the other end of the field.

No doubt about it: their house was ready for them and them only. It wasn't as roomy inside as they thought it would be and they had to crouch down to get in the front opening, but inside felt like nowhere they'd ever been before.

Sniff, said the oldest boy.

They didn't smell anything but the oily and rusty dirt on their own hands.

Listen, said the oldest boy.

They didn't hear anything but the pond water lapping against the old tires.

Look around, said the oldest boy.

Little chinks of light came through some of the cracks and through the front opening, but it was still dark enough that they could feel like they were well hidden.

Perfect, they agreed, hoping no one in the world would notice where they were or what they had been up to.

Acknowledgments

Many of these stories appeared originally in *The Man Who Kept Cigars In His Cap* and *You Know What Is Right*, often in different form. "The Boys' House" appeared originally in *Literary Houses: The Essence of Dwelling*, sponsored by the Seattle Arts Commission and printed, in different form, under the title "A Cathedral of Wishes." "The Man Who Raised Turkeys" appeared originally in the *New York Times*, "Who Had Good Ears" in *Live Music*, "A New Year's Story" and "Buttermilk Pop" in the *Minneapolis Star Tribune*. "Kickers," "The Stray Cat in the Garden," and "Big Boots" originally appeared in *Ploughshares*. "That Could have Been You," "The Robin's Nest," "The Parrot," and "Go to the Ant, Thou Sluggard" appeared in *Georgia Review*.

The Boys' House was designed & set in type by Will Powers at the Minnesota Historical Society Press and was printed by Maple-Vail Press. The typeface is Miller, designed by Matthew Carter.